THE LEGEND
OF
DIDDLEY SQUATT

A Novella from a Brother Fella

Duane Lance Filer

THE LEGEND OF DIDDLEY SQUATT
A NOVELLA FROM A BROTHER FELLA

iUniverse books may be ordered through booksellers or by contacting:

iUniverse
1663 Liberty Drive
Bloomington, IN 47403
www.iuniverse.com
1-800-Authors (1-800-288-4677)

Because of the dynamic nature of the Internet, any web addresses or links contained in this book may have changed since publication and may no longer be valid. The views expressed in this work are solely those of the author and do not necessarily reflect the views of the publisher, and the publisher hereby disclaims any responsibility for them.

Any people depicted in stock imagery provided by Thinkstock are models, and such images are being used for illustrative purposes only. Certain stock imagery © Thinkstock.

ISBN: 978-1-5320-3384-1 (sc)
ISBN: 978-1-5320-3385-8 (e)

Library of Congress Control Number: 2017915094

Print information available on the last page.

iUniverse rev. date: 10/20/2017

Contents

DEDICATION

This book, like many of my previous books, is dedicated to those unfortunate enough to have been born into very difficult situations. Many of us have been bullied because of something deemed awkward by society, something we in truth have no control. Please understand that when brought into this world – each individual living being has absolutely no control of their gender, color, name, height, weight, house address; color of your eyes, hair color; pimpled skin; degenerative health problem, rich or poor – we as newborns have no choice.

So, it us up to each of us, at some point, to understand that WE ourselves have to make our own choices on how to best go forward and to find happiness in our lives. Some of us will find role models; an understanding parent or two; some outreach group of friends/counselors/relatives/co-workers – someone to help us along life's pathway, with hopes that something will "click" and we will become positive and productive in our lives.

I hope this book is one of those "clicks" for you. In the words of my friend Sly Stone, please stand:

Stand
In the end you'll still be you
One that's done all the things you set out to do
Stand
There's a cross for you to bear
Things to go through if you're going anywhere
Stand
For the things you know are right
It's the truth that the truth makes them so uptight
Stand
All the things you want are real
You have you to complete and there is no deal
Stand
You've been sitting much too long
"Stand"

—Sly & the Family Stone

About the Author

My name is Duane Lance Filer and I like to write far out stuff. I grew up in Compton, California and had one of the greatest, richest childhoods one could have growing up in an "inner" city. My mom Blondell Filer lived in Compton until her recent passing in 2016 – living till the end in Compton in the same house me and my six brothers and sisters were raised. I definitely received my artistic genes from Blondell Filer. Love you mom!

My dad Maxcy Filer was involved in the west coast civil rights movement, and during the 60's and 70's I got to witness and was involved in some wild and crazy events during this important time in American history. My family helped integrate the City of Compton, and my dad later served on the Compton City Council for 15 years.

Since birth, I've possessed an extraordinary memory; an insatiable imagination; and a fascination with writing. I started writing in high school, through college, and during my work years.

My first short story was written for Mrs. Pierce's 7th grade English class at Walton Jr. High in Compton. At Compton High School, Mr. Alvin Taylor's Black History class inspired me to write "what you know." My next stop was at Cal Lutheran College (now University) where creative writing professors Ted

LaBrenz and Dr. Jack Ledbetter encouraged me to continue to write my off- the- wall short stories. After college, I continued to learn the craft of writing at the Watts Writers Workshop in 1973-1974 (God bless Harry Dolan); the Open-Door Writers Program for Minority Writers at 20th Century Fox (1980-82): and the Institute of Children's Literature.

I worked for the California Public Utilities Commission (CPUC) for 29 years and retired in 2013. I am and have been married to my beautiful wife Janice for 40 years. My son Lance and daughter Arinn are both bright, ambitious young adults who have made their parents very proud. I have 6 brothers and sisters (Maxine, Kelvin, Anthony, Stephanie, Dennis and Tracy); a goo gaggle of cousins, in-laws and friends.

To date I have self-published 6 books. Following is a brief summary of each book:

1.) "Square Squire and the Journey to DREAMSTATE"

Squire Brooks is a precocious nerd whose only awareness of the transitions in his neighborhood of Compton, California, in the 1960's is the opportunity to chuck stones at the increasing number of For Sale Signs in the yards of his white neighbors. His father's deepening involvement in civil rights creates increasing chaos in his home where Squire writes his short stories and daydreams. Adolescence brings peer-driven lessons about girls, puberty, girls, bullies, and girls as he navigates the temptations during his elementary, junior high, and high school years.

Squire's daydreaming has developed into an imaginative mechanism that frees his mind from all the chaos and allows him to escape to a dream state whenever he writes. After graduating from high school and on a road trip with his dog,

Julius, Squire meets Octavia Steves, who teaches him that his "dream state" is actually a form of meditation/astral projection that could help him become the writer of his dreams.

2.) *"The Baby Boomers First-Hand/First-Year Guide to Retirement.....365 Days of Bliss (???!!!☺ ☺) or Diss (Not???!!! ☹☹)."* – 2014.

Ever wonder what really happens that first year after you retire? I'm talking about the day-to-day emotions, feelings, projects, questions, anxieties....the ups and downs of this very important next step in one's life after some 25/30/35/40 years of formal work?

Well, my *"The First-Hand/First- Year Guide to Retirement.....365 Days of Bliss (???!!!☺ ☺) or Diss (Not???!!! ☹☹)"* could provide some insight for those recently retired or contemplating retirement. This 365 day (from January 16, 2013 to January 16, 2014) 424 page daily journal allows the reader to follow along as I experience the chores, the life; the new budgeting, the wife - the questions, the emotions; some answers and hopefully some solutions.

"First-Hand" is a humorous collection of thoughts and stuff........it does not hit you over the head with heavy retirement statistics such as inflation projections, investment facts, tax shelters, financial formulas, etc...; "musts" the experts tell you that need to be addressed before either retiring or planning your retirement. While this information is indeed necessary, this is not that kind of book – OK? My book is simply a personal essay of my first 365 days of retirement, featuring real names and real people. Included are personal pictures and anecdotes of my 2013 journey that sheds light on the everyday minutia of life.

So no. I am not an expert - just a dude who wrote a one-year journal that I think is informative and will make you stop and think when your retirement time comes. you must have a sense of humor when reading this guide- life is funny and unpredictable. My hopes are that this book/journal will be a source of reference for those of you thinking about retiring, or recently retired. Hey........we are lucky to have made it this far – right?

To change-up and keep the reader interested, the book is broken up into chapters by each month. At the end of each chapter is a "Retire-Recap" of what I learned that month, as well as a "Music Jams of the Month" of my favorite walking/writing songs; and finally, a "Journal Your Journey" section for the reader to jot down any notes/comments/ideas for that particular month.

3.) *Square Squire & the Journey to Dreamstate – Squared Version 2.0 for Teens and Young Adults."* – 2015. This is my 3rd book, a teens and young adult version of my first "*Square* Squire's"book. *Square Squire and the Journey to Dream State – Squared Version 2.0 for Teens and Young Adults,* is a semiautobiographical story of growing up geeky in the last innocent time when all the basketball players had hopes and none of the gangs had guns. **Squared Version 2.0* is a modified version of the original 2012 book where any adult-themed language has been modified and structured for teen and young adult reading*

2015 was a very busy year for me! I self-published my first 3 (three) of a series of 7 (seven) independent children's books from a collection entitled **"LongTALES for shortTAILS."**

Here's a look at these first 3 children stories, all 3 containing eye-popping color illustrations by Jay DeVance III:

4.) ***"Fastjack Robinson"*** - Fastjack was coming to spend the summer with his grandrabbits- Grandpaw and Grandmaw Robinson, in Bunny Junction. Fastjack Robinson had moved to Hare City, but always loved coming back home to visit his beloved grandrabbits as well as his childhood friends House Mouse and Stooley the Pigeon.

After a big welcome-home supper of carrot stew and rabbit tea, Fastjack was informed by the squeaky voiced House Mouse that the notorious, mischievous Grabbit Rabbit was wreaking havoc in Bunny Junction by stealing pies and other carrot items from the families in Bunny Junction.

Little did the Grabbit Rabbit know that, like a young Jackie Robinson, Fastjack Robinson was the fastest rabbit in the world! Somebody in Bunny Junction had to stop the notorious Grabbit Rabbit. So Stooley, House Mouse, Grandpaw, and Grandmaw devised a plan to catch the Grabbit Rabbit. It's Fastjack to the rescue!

5.) ***"Ms. Missy – Bishop's First Dog"*** – Who out there doesn't remember their first pet? Bishop's first dog turns out to be the beautiful diva Missy. Plus, Missy soon has a surprise for the family.

"Ms. Missy – Bishop's First Dog" is a true story concerning my family's first pet – Ms. Missy the diva dog!

Follow along as Bishop, oldest child of the Morrow household, learns the ins and outs of owning and taking care of a dog. Bishop has daily duties of feeding and caring for Ms.

Missy; bathing her in the Morrow backyard with younger siblings Maxine and Kelvin; and training Missy in the ways of the pet and human world. Time passes, as both Missy and the Morrow family grows with additional kids. One day, Missy disappears, and young Bishop feels it is his fault because he scolded Missy too hard. Bishop feels terrible, and fears she has run away for good. When Missy is finally found – she has a surprise of a lifetime for the Morrow family!

6.) ***"Duncan & the Chocolate Bar"*** - The year is 2050. The space shuttle to the moon has been a reality since 2030. There have been scientists, explorers, politicians, entertainers and celebrities; just about every type of scientific type person has been or has plans to go to the moon.........but no ordinary people have been included? Black, white, brown, or yellow....no regular ordinary people have been to the moon. Finally, in 2050, the USA government has decided it is time to send some regular folks to the moon. A contest was held to pick three lucky souls to be sent to the moon. Each person selected could bring a friend. And the best part is that the government claims once the lucky winners get to the moon, there would be a surprise waiting for them.

Young Duncan (Dunk) Sylers,11-years old and from the city of Compton, California, enters the contest. You guessed it – Young Duncan wins and decides to take his younger cousin Drew on the exploration of a lifetime. Follow along as Duncan, Drew, and the other winners (including a wanna-be hippie who brings his parrot as his guest; as well as an aging actress and her equally washed up boyfriend) travel toward the moon. Do they succeed? You'll have to read the book.

Special Thank you for "The Legend of Diddley Squatt – A Novella from a Brother Fella."

Thanks to Pamela L. Sheppard for her encouragement and advice on structure. Pam provided a great roadmap and helped guide me through my early writing progress. Pam has been a trusted friend and a great resource beginning with my first book. Pam can be reached at sheppardedits@gmail.com. Thanks Pam!

Duane can be contacted at 310-413-2947 or preferably at duanelancefiler@gmail.com ; Please visit his website and view his books and paintings at his website (http://duanelancefiler.wix.com/duanelancefiler); or at Facebook or LinkedIn.

PROLOGUE

This is the novel novella exquisite of one Diddley Squatt.

Before delving straight into Sir Didd's life, please allow me to regress and provide a brief statement for those who choose to read this book. Ahem - let me first say this:

"I hope you hep-cats and daddy o's from the 40-s-50's; hippies and squares from the 60's and 70's; nerds from the 80's and 90's; "deemo-CRATS," Re-PUB-lee-cans," in-dee-pen-dents"; southerners and northerners; blacks, whites, browns, yellows, striped, tattooed; Jews and Gentiles, Christians and Muslims alike; Tea-partiers; conservative right-wing alt-righters and liberal-leaning alt-lefters; Black Live Matterers'; foreigners and refugees from every country on this earth; animals and birds/squirrels/dogs and kitties alike from the beginning of time; legal and illegal immigrants; "Dreamers;" fat people, skinny people, tall people, little people, gay people, straight folks; transgender people – everyone/every-being from the 1940's to 2017 - I wish all ya'll will put aside your differences and just enjoy this story about a BULLIED boy all because his name was Diddley Squatt?

When reading, just remember that no one born at birth, from the beginning of time, has control over their color, gender, or birth name (agreed?)

God made us who we are and we had no choice in the matter. Aren't we all just ONE? Enjoy Diddley's journey"

Having said that, let's get it going, shall we?

CHAPTER 1

The Legend is Born

Backwoods Mississippi. Year? Sometime in the mid 1940's early-1950's. Diddley Squatt was born in a rundown section of Rundown City, Mississippi, in a rundown year; a mere afterthought of his mom's latest rundown one-night stands; Rundown's rundown. Diddley's mother, Jackie Squatt, didn't even realize she was pregnant until one of her friends pointed it out:

"My lord, girl, you surely are putting on some weight here lately. How many pork chops you been eating'?"

Jackie's mom, known far and wide as simply Momma Squatt (nobody knew her first name) had very little to say when her only child's pregnancy was finally confirmed.

"Child, now what you gonna do with yo'self now that you went and got yo'self pregnant? You don't know nothing about birthing or taking care of no babies!" said Momma Squatt. "I know I wasn't the greatest momma in the world, but I thought maybe you could one day get that schooling you used to like and get out of Rundown City."

"Momma, it ain't your fault at all. I'm old enough to know what I'm doing. You and daddy Doodley Squatt gave me my schooling, an' I tried, I really did. School just ain't for everybody, and I guess I'm part of that everybody," said Jackie Squatt. "I might be leaving, I just can't stay in Rundown City anymore, and I'm sure you know, no-way I can raise this baby. Could you please, please, PLEASE, raise my child – and maybe one day I can get myself together and be of some good to my child and the rest of the world; and come back and help my son and everybody else?"

"You think I'd abandon my only grandchild?" said Momma Squatt. "I got no other living family but you and your baby. Your daddy Doodley run off and left us. That Doodley wasn't Squatt! Family takes care of family."

So, there it is. At sixteen Jackie Squatt was smart enough to know it was hopeless and she'd be in the way trying to raise a child, so she did indeed split from Rundown City and leave the newborn with Momma Squatt.

Momma Squatt? Momma was the madam of Rundown City's largest hotel/brothel known as "The Copp-A-Squatt Inn." Momma Squatt was a medium sized woman – not overly thin or overly fat – just perfect for a grandma- and she had this pure face with wrinkles ; all in the right spot- that exuded nothing but niceness. She wore glasses, and had graying hair pulled back that often was covered by an ever -present scarf that differed from day to day. Momma Squatt was known by her heart – not by her dress.

Jackie's baby daddy's name was Deangelo – he of African and Italian descent; a very handsome man. During the beginning of the 1900's to the mid-1900's, some French, Spanish, but mainly Italian folks visited Mississippi and settled into some southern U.S. states. They mostly worked in the fishing and canning factories; but some of them were experienced farm workers and worked in the cotton fields;

they moved around like all workers. Deangelo was probably the offspring of one of these early Italian workers; he too abandoned after birth, and just passing through Rundown, looking to find work, when he happened through Rundown City and had the one-nighter with the popular Jackie Squatt. No one ever knew Deangelo's last name. So, when the birth was imminent, the Squatt family tweaked Jackie's father's name Doodley – keeping the beginning "D" to represent both Deangelo and Doodley- to "Diddley" – and left the family name of Squatt – and that was that. Diddley Squatt was the child's name!

Diddley decided later in life that Diddley at least was a better name than Deangelo and Doodley, but not by much; more details on this later.

So there it was. Jackie just felt she had to go her own way or she would not last long on this earth. After giving birth to Diddley with the help of a mid-wife at the Copp-A-Squatt (nothing unusual at all in those days) it was her time to go.

It was a starry night when she left. Moon glistening and the moths and fireflies dancing around the train station's lone lamppost. Jackie boarded a train at Rundown's rundown station, watching as Momma Squatt cradled Diddley in worn swaddling to her bosom. Momma waved to Jackie as the Back-Up-Train Onward left the station.

Momma looked down at young Diddley in the covers; a ladybug landed on his head and Momma swatted him away.

"WOOOOOOOOOOOOOOOOOOOOOOOOOO –WOOOOOOOOOOOOOOOOOOO."

The train whistle screamed as the train slowly rumbled down the tracks. Was that the last time Jackie Squatt would see Rundown City? Was this the last time she would see her sweet baby boy?

"Lord, child! We got our work cut out for us, but we gonna make it," Momma Squatt said as she watched the train slowly pull away.

Life onward. The Copp-A-Squatt Inn sat at the end of a cul-de-sac, a huge house on a block of huge houses nestled in tall pine trees and green shrubs. In the backyards of close-by houses, nothing but trees and forest, rich and green from all the rain.

The Copp-A-Squatt Inn was the major meeting place in Rundown City with all the activity and folks gathered around, always coming and going. The Copp-A-Squatt Inn was part hotel-part brothel. Folks didn't mind. You could rent a room for one night, or a week – even a month. You could partake with one of the ladies – or just stay by yourself and enjoy the music, the food, the vibe of all the happenings- totally up to you. Buicks, Cadillacs, and stylish Oldsmobiles, as well as old beat up jalopies and even some muddy tractors parked around all corners of the shady neighborhood. Mostly black folks lived here in Rundown City; but also a scattering of white folks, either too rooted to the place, or too poor to move when the blacks started moving in, or just plain stuck.

Rundown City was a different place. While most of the citizens were poor, there were also the hep cats in stingy brims, zoot suits, shiny Thousand Eyes and Stacy Adams shoes stepping out of their fancy cars, heading to Copp-A-Squatt's for some good liquor, good music, a domino game or two; bid whist and poker games; but especially to find the big bow-legged women. Saturday nights were a jumpin'!

Momma Squatt's house was massive, an enormous 3 stories tall monster. Walk through the double doors to a wide entry hall, stairs to one side, parlor to the other. A second

4

parlor faced a dining room; the big kitchen and back stairway further on. Momma's quarters were close enough to keep an eye on comings and goings. Upstairs were narrow hallways and small rooms on each side. No need for more than a bed and a washstand here. One grand chamber included a bathtub and private toilet. Smaller toilets were at the end of each of the halls. The third floor had even smaller rooms for the girls to call their own, and a larger room lined up beds in rows. Rooms could rent by the month, the week, or by the hour, whatever was needed.

The kitchen. Momma's good cooking came out of that kitchen; she served neighbors, friends, and clients at her big table. The girls helped and learned Momma's cooking skills; they could cook for everybody and anybody else who stopped by. Mouth-watering aromas of cornbread and black-eyed peas, greens, smothered steak, oxtails, gumbo's, ham-hocks, fried chicken, chitlins, okra, permeated the house and drifted out the doors. Buttery grits and pork chops were the specialty some mornings and Momma Squatt's favorite sweet potato pie and home baked raisin-bread stationed at the opened ground floor windows and sweetened the air throughout the house. The beer and moonshine flowed freely for whoever could pay the price.

Those first 5 years of Diddley's life flew by and he grew to love the house and its various oddities. The massive main floor and tiny upstairs rooms of the Copp-A-Squatt were his playground. The ladies were aunties and sisters to Diddley, taking him willingly when Momma Squatt was busy. They fed him, changed his diapers, played with him, smooched and hugged him endlessly. They all loved that sweet boy.

Diddley grew and stretched out, and soon learned his way around all the nooks and crannies of the brothel. He took to running for the ladies, for towels and linens, for cigarettes from

Momma Squatt's stash. Quick as a cricket, he was. The ladies loved him, the tricks teased him, and he loved them all back. Especially close to "Young Didd" – as he became to be called- were Chastity and Delilah. It just so happened that Chastity and Delilah were 2 of the youngest girls at the Copp-a-Squatt, and easily the most beautiful.

"Come here young Diddley" Delilah would purr in her light musical voice. Delilah had creamy skin and a slim nose that led up to her beautiful green eyes. Her long black hair ran down below her shoulders. She was like a picture painting she was so beautiful. She was Cajun and from the swamps of someplace called "Nah - Awlins', but man, even at such an early age- Diddley could tell Delilah was beautiful.

Diddley would run his little legs over to Delilah and just loved it when she took him into her arms and pulled him up to her warm chest and rocked him in that area. It felt warm and snuggly - like rolling in six or 7 pillows. He loved to snuggle.

"Oh my young Didd, you have the warmest soul, I can just feel it" she would sway with Didd, and Didd would sway right back. He felt SAFE in Delilah's bosom – like squeezing a marshmallow – and even at his early age he knew why men loved to be with her. It was heaven. She was heaven!

Chastity was a different beautiful than Delilah. Chastity was jet black with gleaming white teeth that opened into an irresistible smile that nobody could resist. Chastity had kinkier hair than Delilah- but it was oh so soft and fluffy in the "natural" way that she wore it. She had these cheek bones that she said came from her "Cherokee grandparents;" and these huge brown eyes that just invited you in. Chastity's eyes would pierce through you with their brightness- and then her smile would just explode in your mind and you knew you were safe. She was Cherokee fierce, too, and her attitude often made trouble for her.

"Diddley Squatt… come ovah here and let me hold my Diddley" Chastity would demand with a smile and open arms. She spoke with more attitude than Delilah. Diddley would sprint to Chastity and she would sweep him off his feet and she would hold him tight and squeeze him tight. He could feel the love and strength in this strong black woman from "Cher-o-kee" history. Warm, safe, and loved. That's how these 2 favorite ladies of the night made him feel.

When Diddley wasn't in school he was at the Copp-A-Squatt – working. Young Diddley listened to all the stories around him. Stories of love and betrayal; of miserable failure or glorious success. Sometimes a john left magazines and comic books behind; the ones with pictures of people with no clothes on were weird. These were not his favorites. Diddley loved the superhero comic books left around the best of all. Diddley loved to look at the pictures and his imagination would run wild. He dreamt he could do stuff that other folks couldn't do - like make himself small, or tall, or even invisible. Yeah – he imagined he could crawl up under the door at the Copp-A-Squatt and go sit on a lady's dresser and watch her as she "tricked" the trick into giving her more money than advertised.

Diddley? Diddley was on the creamy side of black, and imagined he could turn himself into any color. He had these huge dimples and the curliest hair ever – and he loved to laugh and be tickled. He would dream of experiments like walking into a store black at first – and see how the owner treated him. Then he would turn his skin white -and watch the owner act totally different towards him. "Young Didd" was a different card, I tell you!

He also imagined that he was one with nature, and could therefore talk to the animals. Diddley loved that Momma Squatt had several animals around the Copp-A-Squatt; there were several dogs running around the enclosed front and back yards. Cats? Momma had stray cats all over the property, and although some of the customers complained, Momma always said, "those cats ain't hurting nobody, they are our friends. God put them here on earth for a purpose to cozy up to you on a cold day... ain't nothing wrong with God's friends-they like family!"

Diddley actually loved talking, rubbing, and smooching with animals more than he liked talking to humans. He imagined one day we would be able to make himself small enough to allow him to ride on the back of dragonflies and soar thru the air; or hang onto the wings of birds and glide. Plus, Diddley loved the green forest outside the yards of Copp-A-Squatt. From time to time, he would sneak outside and sit in the woods. He had a favorite opening in the woods where he would lay on his back and gaze upward, past the tall pines, and just dream his dreams. Diddley loved animals so much, he swore off eating meat at an early age as to not offend any of his animal friends.

Diddley also loved going to church on Sundays. Momma Squatt and the girls got dressed up in their very best, hats hanging from their heads, and climbed into one of Momma's cars, and they always went to church on every Sunday. That preacher guy would get up on the "pulpit" thing and start to itching and pulling up and down... swaying... saying all things about how all needed to pray to God and "sinners' beware. Momma and everybody would be clapping and hollering and shouting "AMEN- THE DEVIL IS A LIAR!" When the musicians started playing and the choir started singing - folks would break out into the aisles of Redeemer Baptist and do this dance called the "holy and happy dance" where they would sway their arms, hucklebuck this way and that; click their heels- point to the heavens and shout "HALLELEJUH" like you wouldn't believe. THE MUSIC WAS DIDDLEY'S FAVORITE PART. These ladies of the choir, and a few men, could sing like you wouldn't believe it. They would sing songs like "You Can't Hurry God" and "His Eye is on the Sparrow" and especially "Do Not Pass Me By"- that song jumped and Didd would get up and be right there with Momma and the girls hollering and singing along. He loved church!

Schooling? Momma Squatt did indeed make Didd go to "Gram-mur" school, which at first he hated, but then learned to love learning about different things and places. He imagined he could fly and experience anything. Although the other kids did make fun of his name, he would always say to himself, quietly, "You don't know Diddley!"

CHAPTER 2

You Don't Know Diddley

So Diddley's mom has split the scene and left the now 2nd grader, 7-year-old Diddley to be raised by Momma Squatt and the other inhabitants of the Copp-A-Squatt Inn. Momma Squatt has enrolled Diddley at Rundown's only elementary/middle school – Rundown Elementary for Kindergarten through 7th grade. From day one, when Momma first walked Diddley into school, Diddley felt like an outcast. He knew he would get teased - just knew it. However, there were also **deeper** reasons that made Diddley feel different – and even excited at the same time.

First off, Diddley had hung around mostly grown-ups during his earliest years – there were very few kids his own age hanging around a brothel. To put it mildly - he was **scared** out of his drawers! Remember, he had no brothers or sisters; no cousins; no people his own age hanging around like most kids. Diddley had mostly talked to johns and the ladies, thus he had no idea how talking to people his own age might be different. This could be a major reason why he felt close to animals – in Diddley's mind they more or less substituted for kids around the Copp-A-Squatt.

Secondly, while Diddley was indeed afraid that first day of school, he also felt excited to be exposed to something different. Finally, he would be exposed to people his own age and hopefully learn what they were thinking. Momma Squatt or the girls wouldn't be there to help him if he had any questions – he would have to figure out stuff on his own and on the spot.

On that first day, Didd was both afraid and excited. He took a seat smack dab in the middle of the school room.

"RIIIIIIIINNNNNNNG"
WENT THE BELL.

"Class. Come to order and take your seats" said Mrs. Fartworthy – Rundown Elementary kindergarten – through 2nd grade teacher. "Now please listen for your name and yell out and raise your hand as I take our year's first day attendance."

Mrs. Fartworthy was this elderly white woman who seemed very nice and caring; although she was a very large woman. She immediately reminded Didd of the lady on the front of the oatmeal box he had for breakfast many mornings. Didd so loved oatmeal, so he had a nice warm feeling toward Mrs. Fartworthy from the very beginning.

Mrs. Fartworthy:	"Jerry Applewood"
Jerry (raises hand):	"here"
Mrs. Fartworthy:	"Cynthia Douglas"
Cynthia (raises hand):	"here"
Mrs. Fartworthy:	"Pryor Richards
Pryor (awkward hand raise)	"Here ma'am" (laughter from kids)
Mrs. Fartworthy:	"Rufus Sommerfield"
Rufus (raises hand):	"present"

| Mrs. Fartworthy: | "Diddley Squatt" |
| Diddley: | "Here" |

THE ENTIRE CLASS BURSTS OUT IN UNCONTROLLED LAUGHTER.

The laughter rattles the walls. The laughter is so loud another teacher passing in the hall rushes in just to make sure things are all-right.

Rufus (laughing):	"Did the teacher say Diddley?"
Cynthia (laughing);	"Yes… with the last name Squatt!"
Full class (laughing):	"What kind of name is that"

LAUGHTER… LAUGHTER…

| Mrs. Fartworthy: | "Alright class… that's enough… settle down. |
| | Mr. Squatt may indeed have a unique name – but nothing is wrong with that. Welcome Diddley." |

Diddley sunk in his seat and wished it would squish into the ground. What a way to start school. As class resumed after attendance, Diddley quickly realized what the upcoming days might look like – that the other students would kid him for several reasons; 1.) of course, his very unique name 2.) cause Diddley had this long curly hair that covered most of his face; 3.) and in time they would undoubtedly learn that he lived at Momma Squatt's Copp-A-Squatt Inn – the brothel in Rundown City.

"RING- RECESS BELL"

The inevitable meeting that first day on the playground; blacktop... near the swings and bars... and indeed it began:

"What kind of first name is Diddley and what kind of last name is Squatt?" laughed Sabrina Tuggars, she one of Rundown Elementary's more well-to-do white students and one of the smartest 2nd graders at school. Nobody messed with Sabrina or the Tuggar's family in Rundown City – they had the biggest and best house. Her father was the Mayor of the small town.

"I dunno... that's my name" said the shy Diddley, "I had nothing to do with my name. Did you of yours?" How else was he supposed to answer?

"I'd be upset if I had a weird name," said Sabrina, "I have a pretty and beautiful name... Sabrina... so I feel pretty and beautiful – and I'm going to be somebody" said the young girl as she twirled her blonde hair and shook it in Diddley's face.

"Plus, my dad is the mayor of this town and we live in the biggest and best house in the city. When the teacher called out your last name "Squatt" – I've heard my daddy talk about that name and that means you have to be related to that place on the edge of town called the Copp-A-Squatt Inn. My dad said that is a bad place, where all the bad men come from all over to get with the bad women who do things for them. So not only do you have the funny name, but you actually live in the Copp-A-Squatt??? Who in heavens knows what kind of stuff goes on there? We need to watch out for this Diddley Squatt boy!""

Other kids then joined in and the insults began:

"Never heard of a kid named Diddley"

"Squatt for a real last name?? Who are your parents?"

"And look at that hair covering his face? What kind of black kid has curly hair like that? (and this from a black kid?)

Diddley felt something strange boiling inside of him like never before. Although shy and quiet, he just couldn't stop what next happened. He got right in Sabrina Tugger's face since she had been the one to make the first insult.

"I don't know much," said young Diddley, then he burst out... "but I know Diddley - and I know I want to be somebody too!"

Sabrina backed off; kind of alarmed that Diddley took up for himself so quickly. If Sabrina was surprised- Diddley himself was shocked at his reaction – but it just came out.

Diddley couldn't say anything else, but he soon learned he didn't have to.

"Diddley is not such a bad name" came a voice weekly from the back of the gathered crowd, "Why do you guys always have to pick on the new people or somebody with a different name?"

"Oh Lord?... only Pryor Richards could say something like that" laughed Sabrina and all the others, "probably the only weirder name and weirder person at this school - Pryor Richards?"

Out from the crowd stepped this weird looking young white kid; freckles on his face, reddish hair, big ears, and not wearing the cleanest of clothes. The others pushed him to the front. Obviously, Pryor was similar to a lot of the Rundown Elementary kids; poor, and one of those few white families still stuck in Rundown City.

He stuck out his hand to Diddley.

"'Nice to meet you Diddley Squatt – my name is Pryor Richards."

Diddley was surprised. He had never shaken a white person's hand before, but was happy and surprised that someone his age stuck up for him and was being nice to him.

"Nice to meet you Pryor. I like your freckles" said Diddley as he shook Pryor's hand and they immediately bonded.

"Two misfits - what a mess" said Sabrina as she and her other friends shook their heads in disgust and walked off.

Diddley had made his first friend; and as usual for Diddley, it was an unusual find - a white friend!

When Diddley got home that night, he went through his usual routine. Chores, then dinner with Momma and the girls at the big table in the dining room. Afterwards as the dishes were being moved from the table, some of the girls asked him how his first day went. He didn't bring up the episode of attendance and the laughing about his name. He just didn't think it was worthy to bring up.

"Fine" he said half-heartedly while brushing some crumbs off the table.

Later that night at bedtime, Didd brushed his teeth as usual; climbed into bed, and assumed he would fall asleep just as every other night of his life. However, he found himself tossing and turning as he tried to go to sleep. He just couldn't fall asleep as usual tonight?

Finally, after wrestling with himself to no end, he sat up in bed and said aloud:

"Why can't I fall asleep?" Diddley directed his tirade at the left corner of his small room where a spider regularly spun his nightly web. Didd had never even looked the spider's way before.

"So Mr. Spider, you've been here forever. Why can't I fall asleep?" said Didd with his arms propped behind his head and the pillows - looking up at the ceiling.

"Well… don't blame me or my web!" Didd swore he heard the comment coming from the spider? "I don't make a sound when spreading my nightly web. Spiders are the quietest insects known to man."

WHAT?

Diddley looked in the spider web's direction and said "Did Didd just hear a spider speak?"

"You humans never cease to amaze me- for some reason you think humans are the only intelligent living beings God put on this earth. You don't think the rest of us so called "animals" can communicate? What foolishness? You and I have just communicated haven't we… do you need to see lips move? Hell naw – my lips are so tiny you couldn't see them anyway? But we did we just communicate – didn't we Didd? Just go with it my young friend. So keep going… you've got me curious… even though you may not think we are talking… why is it that you can't sleep?"

"Ok Mr. Spider, I'll play along. I can't go to sleep because today was my first day of school; and all the kids laughed at my name when it was called during attendance call. You probably already know name is Diddley Squatt. and I love my name. What's wrong with my name? And then at recess, this girl named Sabrina Tuggars – who is the mayor's daughter – said I should be ashamed for several reasons; first off because of my funny name; and then because I live here at the Copp-A-Squatt. What's wrong with the Copp-A-Squatt Mr. Spider? You live here? Oh… and another thing… a black kid said I had different hair and should be ashamed of my hair? Does this happen to every kid on their first day of school?"

"Calm down Diddley… calm down," said the spider, "I can see you've got a lot to learn. I've been in many a bedroom, kitchen, dining room -.and I've heard a lot. Humans can be mean – especially little kids who overhear stuff from their crazy parents. What happened was you were maybe HURT for the very first time in your life... because of what the kids said. I've heard stories about your good loving heart – and this may have been your initial hurt. But I am here to tell you it won't be the first time you'll be hurt, so you have to deal with it and get over it."

Diddley sits up in bed.

"Yeah... you could be right. I've heard some of the girls say they've been "**HURT**" by some of their friends, but I've never had this feeling of hurt before. I have to tell you hurt hurts! I have been so lucky I guess. Momma Squatt; the ladies, the guys - Copp-A Squatt Inn has shown me nothing but love and I guess this may be one of my first outside learning experiences. It is becoming a little clearer. Yeah, when they were laughing at me, it was the first time I didn't feel loved; and nobody was there to take up for me. But this kid named Pryor Richards came up later and I met my first white friend."

"Sounds like an eventful day. You've had quite the learning experience, and now it sounds like you are realizing many whys and learning some lessons like why they talked about you, and why you didn't immediately lash out (because you were not brought up that way); and most importantly why you can't sleep tonight; and why you've... ahem... interrupted me from spinning my nightly web. But I forgive you. This was indeed your first experience with hurt and nastiness," said Mr. Spider.

"I guess this is an important lesson learned," said Diddley, "people will think one thing just because it is said – but that doesn't make it the truth. You must walk in other people's shoes to really know what they see, feel and go through. Yeah... so thank you Mr. Spider. I feel much better! Yes -hurt hurts – but understanding why the hurt; and who/why the hurt comes from – if misguided and unfair- you then have to learn to just move on and learn from the experience. I know I could never be on the other end and hurt somebody like those who called me out -it doesn't make sense." Diddley eased back down into the comfort of his covers and pillows.

"Glad to help you young Diddley. Sounds like you've worked out something in that human head of yours," said Mr. Spider

"How can I ever repay you?" said Diddley.

"You don't owe me anything... glad to help," said Mr. Spider. "Well... maybe you can. Next time you hear a girl screaming about "come get this spider" YOU can come running and just catch my brother spider on a piece of paper and take him outside to the woods. Tell others they don't have to just squish spiders; just put a piece of paper up and we will crawl on the paper and take us outside and we will make new homes outside; or maybe one day come back inside and spread" Mr. Spider let out a laugh.

I'll "spread" the word," said Didd with a laugh. He then let out a long yawn. Now he was indeed sleepy because his mind had been cleared.

Diddley fell into a peaceful sleep.

So Diddley's time through Rundown Elementary passed quickly. Overtime, most of the kids respect him and leave him alone because he is so shy and quiet, and because Pryor stepped forward and welcomed him. Pryor and Diddley became friends – although they kept it quiet. Pryor said his parents weren't that kindly to black folks; and even Diddley had no idea how the Copp-A-Squatt folks might react to him having a close white friend. However, as fate quickly showed, there were bullies at every school and Rundown was no exception. If Didd thought Sabrina Tuggars was mean, he was about to learn she wasn't alone and others could be tougher.

One such figure showed up soon – guy's name was Herbert Hebert. You would think with such a unique name, he'd be the last one bullying somebody – but with his size nobody would dare.

Oh no. Herbert Hebert.

"Diddley Squatt? What kind of a name is Diddley Squatt? Both Diddley and Squatt are sissy names" said the one and only Herbert Hebert.

Herbert was the tallest kid in Rundown Elementary; a 7th grader; must have been close to 6ft. tall in elementary school. Herbert was certainly oblong, but he wasn't any type of physical specimen himself. He had long awkward legs that led to his feet which jutted outward- he was the opposite of pigeon-toed- he was what they called "slew-footed." I swear... standing still- Herbert looked like the coatrack that hung inside the corner of our teacher, Mrs. Fartworthy's, classroom.

Herbert looked like a coat hanger on stilts; plus, he had beaver teeth that were two sizes too big for his mouth. I bet he could chew through bone; and pimples? Child had pimples all over his face; face looked like the dirt road leading up to Momma Squatts! Here he is looking like Bucky Beaver, but because he's bigger than most of the teachers, he had the nerve to bully people? But that's what life gives you... you gotta get through it.

So Diddley took his bullying. Took the other kids calling Momma Squatt "Momma Twat" and all kinds of names. What could he do? Diddley was still fairly a little runt – but all of

Momma Squat's girls said he would one day be "one of the finest men to walk the earth."

He had that creamy colored skin and huge dimples, but it was the hair that all the girls liked. The curls had curls... had curls... had curls. He didn't even need any pomade or anything; the curls just sat on the top of my head and along his cheeks - and the girls just loved to run their fingers through that hair.

One day his new secret friend Pryor asked him if he needed help dealing with Herbert, but Diddley told him thanks but no thanks- it was his fight and he would figure out how to deal with this bully. Pryor was a good friend for the offer though.

One day at the Copp-A-Squatt, as he was sulking around and cleaning one of the girl's rooms – the room of one Priscilla Hotbody (she was one of grandma's newest best girls - shaped like a beautiful coke-bottle- and walked like she owned the earth... Priscilla was fine as wine!) one of her johns who everybody called Nate the Skate, pulled Didd aside and said "What's wrong with you son," saying he could tell something was wrong. Nate was a different dude; wore skates and skated everywhere he went in rundown city – and he was good. Somebody said if he was white he could've made the U.S. Olympic skating team. I asked around and learned that roller skating was not even an Olympic event. Anyway, Nate was also known as a pick-pocket. He had fast hands and could reach into your pocket without you even realizing it; but he only did that if he didn't like you. In addition to skating and having quick hands, Nate also held a harmonica in his mouth and played the harmonica as he skated. Nate could do twists and turns... skate backward/sideways... all while playing that harmonica in his mouth.

"What's wrong young Didd?' said Nate.

Didd hesitated, but for some reason deeply trusted Nate. Who wouldn't trust a grown man on skates?

"Herbert Hebert at school has been talking about me and Momma Squatt… calling me a "sissy" and Momma bad names I don't want to repeat. Yesterday, he said I better give him my lunch money or he was gonna punch me in my face" he said to Nate. Although Didd wasn't a big talker, he felt good and comfortable talking to Nate who had initiated the conversation.

"Son-of-a-bitch!' cursed Nate. I was used to curse words… although as I said Momma Squatt said I was never to repeat them. "Diddley, this Herbert guy is messin' and bullying you – and I can't sit by and let that happen. Lawd knows what any of the other johns would say if you told them. We all love you equally, but some of the other johns are some badass people. The thing with bullies is YOU have to confront them… no one else can do it for you. So please keep what I am about to suggest to you quiet, keep it on the "down low" as they say, and I swear in a few days I will help you out and we will fix this chump Herbert Hebert and his insults will stop," said Nate.

Diddley nodded, promising not to tell.

A couple of days passed. Diddley was twitching; wondering what Nate's idea would be to stop Herbert's bullying. Herbert was still on the attack, and now started to bring his posse with him.

Then, one morning when Didd was in the kitchen eating breakfast (Diddley loved oatmeal or just cornflakes and milk-simple and light), Nate walked in and said he had a plan. They sat across from this humongous, black stove that was the centerpiece of Momma Squat's kitchen. This thing was huge and black, and was used constantly to cook all the meals in the house. Nate pulled Diddley to him and whispered in his ear:

"Sssssssssssssssssssshhhhhhhhhh, young Didd. I've got somethin' good for you. Meet me out back in about five minutes, OK?"

"Ok Nate, I got it." Diddley was curious. What did Nate have planned?

When Diddley met Nate in the backyard, Nate was without his skates on. Nate threw his arm around Diddley as they walked into the woods.

"Ok… here's what we are gonna do… but first you got to listen to my little story that goes like this:

"When I was a little boy, my grandfather sat me on his knee, pulled out a "har-mon-ee-car" and said:

"Little Nate- this is the cheapest musical instrument that our slave masters used to give to us; and it's easy to learn to play. All over the south Negros played the harmonica in cotton fields and everywhere where the master had us working. The harmonica sound is easy to the ears and you can feel the soul of the music. Also, we played certain songs on the harmonica to alert the rest of the slaves that master was close- so you had to watch out. I am giving you the best give I can- my special harmonica"

"See Didd, like my grandfather told me -I think the harmonica has special powers for black folks. We used it for all kinds of signals. I want to give you my grandfather's special harmonica; I don't need it anymore- ain't nobody gonna mess with Nate the Skate!" said Nate.

Nate removed a small harmonica from his pocket. It hung on a round chain – big enough to fit around Diddley's neck, which is where he placed it.

"Diddley, you play on this harmonica anytime that bully is messing with you – like the slave masters back in the day. I'll teach you a couple of tunes that will scare the "heebee jeebies" out of that Herbert Hebert and you will be freed."

"I'm going to teach you some easy songs on this here harmonica right quick. The first song I'm going to teach you is called "I Put a Spell on You." It's an old blues song I've been playing for years, and this is the song I want you to play first for your bullying friend.

Nate took out another bigger harmonica for him, and they each placed their harmonicas to their mouths. They practiced the song which had some spooky... spooky notes that went high and low, it was definitely a scary song. After about an hour's practice, Diddley had the song down.

"Ok... you got it down good enough. Now, take this box – DON'T LOOK IN IT OR OPEN IT – until the next time you see Herbert. Here's what you tell him (Nate got down and whispered in Diddley's ear again.) Diddley's eyes got BIG from what Nate was telling him, and he looked at Nate with a big smile on his face.

Next day at school Herbert Hebert came up to Diddley on the playground. He towered over Didd and said "You got my lunch money, sissy?" Herbert danced around Diddley, chanting, "Your mama didn't want you, your mama threw you away, #$$% bastard boyyyyy..."

Herbert's taunts drew a crowd; all the kids circled around Diddley and Herbert.

Diddley calmly pulled out his harmonica and looked Herbert dead in the eye.

"I'm puttin' a spell on you, Herbert Hebert."

"What?" said Herbert. "What you talkin' about, you little sissy runt?"

Diddley started blowing his "I Put a Spell On You" tune on the harmonica, stopping between refrains to repeat, "I'm puttin' a spell on you, Herbert, and you kids are all witnesses!"

Didd pointed to the crowd gathered around as he picked up playing again.

"You crazy, Diddley Squatt. I'm gonna beat your ass good," snarled Herbert.

"Listen to this." Diddley got right up close to Herbert and up to Herbert's ear. Without anyone noticing, in his other hand he opened the box Nate had given him, and reached behind Herbert's ear lickity-split, like Nate had taught him. Didd waved his hand slowly in front of Herbert's face. "I'm puttin' a spell on you. You better leave me alone."

THEN EVERYBODY SAW IT.

Something hairy reaching out from behind Herbert's ear. A HUGE TARANTULA SPIDER started to crawl across his face.

ALL THE KIDS SCREAMED!

"I PUT MY SPELL ON YOU," yelled Diddley, "and if you ever mess with me again, next time it'll be a snake!"

Well, Herbert started shaking, screaming and jumping, hitting at his head trying to knock that tarantula off. Herbert got so spooked he peed his pants. All the kids laughed and laughed, some rolling on the ground laughing. Herbert ran off.

All the kids gathered around Diddley, cheering and slapping him on the back. Diddley was never bullied by Herbert Hebert again; nor was any other kid for that matter.

From that day on, Diddley was never without his harmonica. Ms. Chastity threaded a thin piece of leather in between the links of the old chain and knotted it in the back so that the necklace hung perfectly around Diddley's neck. The harmonica was with Didd and Didd was with the harmonica.

After the Herbert Hebert episode Diddley definitely knew he might be different.

CHAPTER 3

Diddley's Early Unique Experiences

Number One

Didd sat on the back porch of the Copp-A-Squatt the summer before he started 8th grade at Rundown Elementary/Middle School – only one more year left before he started high school. He was now at the end of 12 years old, nearing 13-years; just sitting on the porch looking out into the back woods with his trusty harmonica in his mouth – playing this old blues tune known as "Squirrel Meat Stew" he had picked up. These old houses really never had any back fences, and backyards just ran out into the woods. This was good, because deer, possums, raccoons, and rats - all these different animals would run up to the end where the brown grass part ended – and you could bond with the animals. Didd loved to just sit on the porch and watch the animals; plus, when nobody was looking, he would rumble through the trash bin where Oscar (one of Momma's house men others called a "pimp") and the other help would throw the garbage after eating. Didd would dig through the trash and get the leftovers, squish them in a paper bag, and place it out on the edge of the backyard/woods area. He'd sit there and watch the animals come eat. They loved the food. Then, one day, something really strange happened?

As he was putting some of the leftovers out on the rickety back fence for the animals – today he put out some pork-chop bones, some un-eaten grits, some egg remnants, burnt toast… - just laid it across the fence, when this possum came up and acted like he wasn't scared at all. To young Didd's amazement, the possum started talking:

"Thanks young Diddley. All the animals have been watching you from afar and we appreciate all the food you bring out here to us. It all tastes good and so keep it coming."

"Possum's can't talk," Didd said.

"Why not? Why can't we?" said the possum, "you humans just think we can't talk because you can imagine the trouble we would be in if humans knew we could talk. We just choose not to talk. But to some few humans that we feel comfortable with – we will talk. Diddley Squatt, you are one of the few humans we feel comfortable talking. My friends will talk to you, you'll see."

"Wow" said young Diddley. "I love all animals. I really like animals more than people. Animals always let you know how they feel."

"You're welcome" said the possum. "My name is Percy Possum, and I've been hanging back here in Momma Squatt's backyard for years. Lots of action at this whorehouse, so there is always a lot of extra discarded food in the garbage. I hope we can be friends." Percy extends his free hand while holding onto his food with the other.

Young Diddley had witnessed this before from the johns, the importance of the shaking of hands, and knew he must respond. So, he shifted over to the back of the fence and shook Percy's free hand. The bond was set!

Before he left, Percy said "you don't happen to have any fresh food on you young Didd- do you?"

"I have my lunch, a tomato sandwich. Sorry, but I don't eat meat. I could never eat something that once breathed like me. One of the johns said that makes me a "ve-gee-tarian." You are more than welcome to my sandwich" said Didd as he pushed the sandwich into Percy's paws. Percy swished his tail in happiness.

"Thanks" said Percy," contrary to what you might think, we possums and animals sometimes like fresh food. I can share this fresh tomato sandwich with the rest of the animals. As for your eating habits, humans and animals aren't much different. Take us possums - we eat just about anything – but we even have a few "vegetarians" that I'm aware. I knew you were special; and keep playing that harmonica - we animals sense something magical when we hear you playing. See you later young Diddley," said Percy, "I'm sure we will be talking more in the future. Like I said, you are one of the exceptional ones."

Percy slowly crept back into the woods; his teeth holding the bag of discarded food and the tomato sandwich bag in his hands.

"Wow!' was all Diddley could say.

Number Two

One day Diddley was told to go up to one of Momma's rooms and run an errand for one of the john's who everybody called GG Prince. GG was called a "musician" and played this instrument everybody called a "gee-tar." Diddley got up to the room, walked in on GG and Rosella who was slung across the bed with a big beautiful smile on her face; GG sitting on a chair, gently strumming his guitar.

"Hey young buck, I need some grease to grease my guitar strings for my show later on tonight. The best grease is that old grease behind Momma Squatt's stove in the kitchen. You gotta get down real low and reach well under that old stove for the best grease. Young buck – you think you can get ol' GG some good grease?" said GG. GG had this huge brown face, with bubbles (pimples) scattered throughout his cheeks, chin and forehead; and when he smiled he had a gold tooth that sparkled on the right side of his mouth. His graying hair was pushed straight back, and he reeked of that strong "cologne" stuff.

"I can do that for you sir" said young Diddley. Diddley flew down the hallway, past the other rooms with the doors open and the girls and johns hanging out in their t-shirts, bras, stockings, etc… smoking and rubbing around, music and smoke drifting from the rooms in the dark.

Diddley got down to the empty kitchen and there was the enormous coal black stove he was sure GG was talking about. Diddley learned about "the stove" at an early age – he had pressed his finger against it once when he was crawling around, and he quickly learned what the word "hot" meant. "Hot" was no joke! This thing looked like a huge black monster from some comic book; two big burners in the front - two in the back -a huge stovepipe running from the back middle to the top of the ceiling. If it was on a train track, it could probably run you over. If you brushed up against it; grease would rub off against your skin. It was a steel animal!

So Diddley is in the kitchen looking at this thing.

"There's no way I can move this stove," he said to no one in particular. He gets down on his knees and peers up under – he can see some squishy, slurpy liquid stuff which he assumes is grease, but it is right in the center of the floor – about 2 feet from each end of the stove.

"I can only get to that grease if I was the size of a mouse or a small bug and could crawl under. How is that ever going to happen," thought Didd.

"*Think Diddley. Think Diddley Squatt!*" Diddley says as he starts tapping his fingers against his forehead, trying to knock some ideas into it. He then moved his tapping fingers to his chest, and his fingers inadvertently tapped against his harmonica.

Wait! Didn't Nate say his grandfather told him he swore the harmonica was a magical instrument? Didd held up his harmonica and looked closely, and saw it had exactly 10 blow holes- ranging from hole # 1 on the left (the lowest note) all the way to hole number 10 on the far right (the highest note.)

"*What would happen If I could hear these notes separately and make a strong wish?*" Diddly pursed his lips and blew hard directly into the middle # 5 hole while wishing "I wish I was smaller... I wish I was smaller!!!" Nothing happened. The sound was muffled.

Didd tried blowing on #10 – a high, clear note floated out. Still nothing. He tried the #3; the #7, the #9. Nothing. He then shook the harmonica and dust and spit flew from the holes. He then blew #3 again and wished "smaller!!!!!!!!"

SWOOOOOOOOOOOOOOSH

Suddenly he felt dizzy, and looked up and saw the ceiling growing farther away; and when he quickly looked down, it was just the opposite -the ground was coming closer? Before he knew it, he was eye level with the top of the table.

"GOOD GOLLY MISS MOLLY!" said Diddley, shouting a phrase he had heard in a song. He looked around to see if anyone had seen him shrink. The room was quiet, nobody was in the kitchen or just outside in the hall or in the stairwell - only the usual bumping noises from the rooms upstairs.

"I wonder what happens if I blow hard and wish hard- into the smallest, lowest number # 1 hole. Here goes… "make me smaller" wished Didd.

BLOW!!!!

And once again the floor closes closer and the ceiling gets farther. Now- Diddley is level with the bottom legs of the stove and could see under the stove? Diddley looked around and it was undeniable.

Diddley had shrunk to the size of a mouse???

"OH WOW!!!' exalts Diddley," I imagined it and it came true. I made myself smaller just by tapping my head 3 times and playing the smallest numbered hole on my 'monica - imagining it? Can others do this?" Diddley says to himself as he steps under the stove and moves toward the grease. He finds an old beer bottle cap and slides it toward the grease spot. He then locates an old potato chip that has hardened; maneuvers it under the grease like a shovel, and begins scooping grease into the bottle cap. When the cap is full, he slides the cap along the greasy floor and it easily slides to the end of the stove. He then empties the cap, and pushes it back and fills it again with the potato chip; he does this a couple more times; each time emptying the bottle cap at the entrance – until he figures he has enough grease for GG. He is then left standing next to the stove, wondering what to do next, and most importantly, how is he going to get back to his natural size?

"Oh well" he says. He starts tapping his forehead like before and says "I wish I was big again… I wish I was big again" He blows the #8 hole, one of the HIGHEST notes on his 'monica.

SWOOSH!

He looks up and the ceiling starts getting closer; and when he looks down, it is just the opposite; the floor starts moving farther away. Soon he can tell he is his old height again.

"Jeez - how did this happen? God must have special plans for me? I can make myself small or big; probably even bigger too, just by tapping my forehead 3 times and playing different holes on my trusty harmonica.

Now his regular height, Diddley puts all the scooped grease into a big cup, cleans up the mess, and heads up the stairs to GG's room. GG is thrilled he got his grease. What a night.

Number Three

One night, some time (but not much) after the smalling incident, Didd sat in his bedroom looking out the window, listening to the critters and the crickets. He thought to himself – If I can talk to some animals and make myself smaller, who knows what else I could do?

Didd's mind drifted to how he loved to listen to all the conversations going on at the Inn. The Copp-A-Squatt brought in men of all types: there would be businessmen in suits who came from the nearby big cities just for the night to partake of the ladies; I heard many of them say they were married and their wives' "weren't treating them right"- so they had no other choice but to come to Momma Squatt's; there were everyday farm workers who worked in the cotton, wheat, and corn fields or the nearby factories; there were gangsters and hustlers in zoot suits and fancy shined shoes so clean you could eat off of em'; men of all types; even some "pol-a-tish-ends" (politicians) and the "po-po" (police); white officers - they all came to Momma's because she had some caring ladies. Didd would listen to all their conversations, cuz he imagined they all thought he was too young to understand what they were talking about; not-knowing he was always a great listener and had a great memory. He heard some good stuff. But what he remembered best and learned from all the listening was it was better to be nice to people and get along — and this helped make life easier.

He remembered one saying that really, really stuck in his mind and summed it all up for him — "Be nice to people and make it work, and be fair."

The ladies and the johns would sometimes play games after the johns "had done their business" and were maybe waiting for the next bus or train. They would play word and mind games and talk about crazy stuff. One day Chastity asked Diddley, "Young Didd, if you had one superpower in the world like a Superman or Batman, what would you like your superpower to be?

Diddley thought for a minute, and of course didn't divulge his already known powers of talking to animals or making himself small, no way. He thought of something that most people might think of as a superpower.

"I'd like to be able to fly" he said. "I'd like to fly high in the sky and look down on this earth and see all the beauty that God has made from up above."

Chastity and the girls and johns/everybody who overheard burst out laughing.

"You would choose to fly as your wish?" said Cecil the Beetle; this every weekend john who had huge ears and gapped teeth- and indeed looked like a beetle in his green suit.

"Hell… why wouldn't you choose to be the Invisible Man where you could walk into a bank and walk out with all the money without anybody seeing you? Or as the Invisible Man, you could walk into beautiful womens' bedrooms all over the world and watch them naked. Fly? Are you nuts?" asked Cecil the Beetle.

"That would be wrong" Didd said, "I don't need to steal anybody's money or see anybody naked unless they want me to see them. Why do people have to cheat to be happy? I don't need to do wrong - it would make me unhappy. I like nature and calm stuff and I want to help people and make the world a better place," Diddley said testily.

Chastity and all the folks laughed. But then Chastity said "that was really sweet Didd… and I'm glad you feel that way. Going to those early Sunday School classes at Rundown Holy Redeemer First Baptist Church of the Saints really paid off. You are one special kid and keep those good God thoughts; stay positive," she said as she reached down and kissed Didd on the top of his head. Her perfume smelled really good.

"Niggas pul-eese," said Cecil, "you got to git while the getting's good. C'mon young blood -wish you could fly instead of being invisible?" Cecil pulled out a flask of whiskey and took a sip.

Cecil the Beetle and Chastity had no idea that Didd already had the ability to make myself small- and had already had one episode of talking to animals. Of course, he could never tell anybody about what he had experienced. NEVER!

So Diddley just sat back and listened as they talked some more, as they passed this smelly smelling cigarette around. He had smelled it before -they called it either a "joint" or "mary-wanna." They all continued to discuss that Diddley said he would pick being able to fly over being invisible; some for and some against. Laughter continued.

Didd, exhausted, finished his chores and once again went and sat out on the back porch. This was easily his best place to sit after working and just think about things.

Didd was sitting there with his torn blue jeans on (he loved blue jeans), some second-hand boots; striped socks that Nate the Skate had given him -torn –t-shirt; curly hair blowing in the nice Rundown City breeze; and, of course, his trusty new best friend harmonica around his neck as always.

He felt something light on his left hand. He looked down and indeed a ladybug had landed on his left hand. Didd reached down to shoo him off;and indeed he shoo-ed him off; but then, Didd felt the bug land again; and the insect did this a couple of times. He felt, without a doubt, that this particular ladybug was doing what they called "messing with him." So, since he didn't like to harm living things, Didd raised his hand and took a long look at this ladybug on his hand and said "what do you want? Why won't you fly away ladybug?"

"You must be one stupid human! Percy the Possum said you were special – the "anointed one" he said." The ladybug ruffled its wings, obviously annoyed. "They are not properly smart if they think you are the anointed human they sent me all the way out here to find."

"What? Did you just say something?" Didd said as he raised his arm right up to his face and closely got up in the ladybug's face.

"Yes -that was me talking" said the ladybug, now a little bit spooked and frightened that she had gotten Didd's attention, however her voice was still stern.

"Who are you?"

"I, sir, am Lady M. Bugg" said the ladybug while fluttering her eyes and her wings at the same time. "Percy the Possum said you understood animal speak. I guess he was right."

"You're a girl?" asked Didd.

"I am indeed a lady! Ms. Lady M. Bugg. They call me LadyM. The M is for Mademoiselle" said the ladybug. "You don't have anything against lady creature's, do you?"

"I didn't mean to upset you" said Didd," I like all animals. Let's start again. My name is Diddley Squatt," said Diddley as he stood up and bowed to Lady M.

"Thank you young squire Diddley" said LadyM, "I understand you have this major wish to fly. Is that correct?"

"Yes ma'am. I would love to fly high in the sky and see the world from above" said Diddley, " How did you know?"

"We insects are everywhere; we hear all -believe me!" said LadyM. LadyM thought for a while, rubbed her antenna together, and continued:

"And sir, how do we proceed?" she said as she fluttered her wings and finally flew up from Diddley's arm. She flew high up into his face and looked directly into his eyes.

"Well, I already have the ability to make myself small by playing the #1 hole on my harmonica – so that's a start" said Diddley.

"What?" said Ms. Lady Bugg, "we insects, like all animals, love music -let me see you do it."

Didd then pulled the harmonica to his mouth, pursed them over the low # 1 note; said the requisite wish of "please make me small" – blew the harmonica hard as he could at the low note; blew like a gust of cold wind.

BLEWWWWWWLOWWWWWWWWWWWW

Once again, the ground enlarged and the sky fell away… and soon he was looking up and could tell he was actually a little smaller than LadyM.

"Blew that baby hard" said Didd" I'm even smaller than before.

"Wow! Climb on my back, and let's go for your first ride" said LadyM, very impressed.

"Let's go!" said an excited Diddley as he climbed up LadyM's spindly leg and was soon sitting dead center on LadyM's back. He tethered his harmonica rope around some appendages jutting from the ladybugs back – and he was ready to ride!

Ms. Lady Bug flashed her eyelashes up and down and some lights came on; just like he imagined headlights on an airplane might react. Diddley held on tight.

"Ready for lift-off" said LadyM as Didd heard a slight sound like a motor starting up and he could feel his butt humming from the engine as LadyM's body fired its insect igniting system. Soon, he could tell it was time…

"RRRRRRRRRRRRRRRRRRRRRRRRRRRRRRRR"

LadyM took to the air! They first hovered like a helicopter for a while. Then – zoom -LadyM took off and banked sharply to the left past the Copp-a-Squatt -in-between trees, not less than an arms-length from Diddley's face! Zooming in and out between the trees; up high into the air, as Didd made sure to stay in the dead center/middle of LadyM's coal black rump to avoid the fire-engine red flapping wings that were chirping at lightning speed!

"Are you okay Mr. Diddley Squatt?" asked LadyM as she banked around the trees and shrubs in the forest, occasionally flying high above the trees so Didd could get a good grasp of how high and low they could fly.

"I'm having a great time!" said Diddley excitedly, as the wind swept through his teary eyes and he had to be careful to keep his head tilted down from the force of the wind, or he might be knocked from his perch. He thought to himself, should I ever get another flight, it might be a good idea to bring some type of goggles.

As they flew around, Didd tried to capture these moments in his memory. It was a wonderful ride, banking in and out and about. He wasn't scared one bit- he always wanted to know what flying felt like. The earth down below was so beautiful and peaceful... no human talk or thoughts to disturb the scenery. Just life below. And the smell? Pine trees; sweet birch trees; fern; wild garlic; salmonberry - it was like heaven. It appeared time stood still as they soared and roared. LadyM stopped at the top of a tree that had to be a hundred feet tall -right on a leaf- and it allowed Didd to look down into the beautiful forest and canyon below. The air was so still and sweet; he imagined this was what heaven must have been like. Didd was one lucky soul!

LadyM said this initial flight would end soon. She flew back to the Copp-A-Squatt backyard and parked on the back fence where no one could see.

"We must do this again young Didd; I must say as a lady flight captain you were a model passenger for an initial flight," said LadyM as I climbed off her back.

"This was one of the greatest days of my life!" Didd told her, "Yes, let's do this again. Thank you!"

She revved up her engines and departed in a flash. Didd blew #10 BIG hole on his harmonica and was soon his regular size again.

What a day!!

Young Didd's elementary/middle school years were drawing to a close. He was happy. No more bullying. He loved school -loved playing the harmonica.

At this point in his life he had discovered at least why he was exceptional. He could talk to animals. He could make himself small. And, he could fly.

Unfortunately, the very next morning, Didd learned a lesson important in life- that happiness could be followed with sorrow. He was told to come to the door; that he had a visitor. When he got to the door, there stood one of his main/bestest friends, Pryor Richards. Pryor had never had the nerve to come to the Copp-A-Squatt door alone; his family would have killed him.

Pryor told him that his family would be moving out of state after the upcoming Rundown Elementary/Middle School graduation exercises. Pryor's dad had gotten a job up north somewhere and they would be moving out of Rundown City. Diddley then told Pryor to meet him in the woods behind the Copp-A-Squatt on the day before Pryor left. The two had been friends for 6/7 years.

On the day before Pryor left, Didd and Pryor met, alone, in the woods.

"You will always be my first friend" said Diddley to Pryor as they sat on stumps in the beautiful woods; squirrels and birds flitting around.

"You were always there for me Diddley; just having a friend to talk to was special -and a black friend at that "said

Pryor as he chucked Diddley on the shoulder and they both laughed.

"I know. I knew early on from my animal friends that God doesn't care what type of living being you are – we are all one – but you were my first friend and took up for me, even though you are white" – he chuckled and chucked Pryor back on his shoulder. The two laughed.

"Maybe one day we can get back together, and hopefully it won't have to be in secret out in the woods" said Pryor.

"For sure. The world is moving fast and hopefully in a better direction. I'm positive one day we will meet again my friend."

Diddley and Pryor hugged.

Time to move on.

CHAPTER 4

High School Years

So Didd graduated from Elementary/Middle School. Next up were his high school years. Didd was entering the 9th grade. High school in Rundown City ran from, 9th, 10th, 11th, and 12th grade years. Didd was now in his 9th grade year -just started his teen years at 14 years old.

Diddley's first class at Rundown High was Math. Diddley was sitting in the middle of the classroom as the teacher called the roll. When the teacher called out "Diddley Squatt" of course laughter and catcalls cascaded from the room – but Diddley was used to it and it didn't bother him at all. He just raised his hand and said "here" and everything quieted down. As the teacher continued roll-call through the "S's" and "U's and got to the "V's" – Didd's ears perked up when the teacher called out the name "Marco Valentus."

"Here" came a voice behind Diddley. When he turned around he saw this fair/light skinned lad – about Didd's same height and weight – and they smiled at each other. Marco had these sparkling green eyes and curlier hair than Diddley. Strange? Marco wasn't white-white, and he definitely wasn't black. He was kind of in-between?

After class, in the hall, as the students were milling about before the next bell – Diddley just felt he had to meet this Marco. He found him walking down the hall and went up to him and said:

"My name is Diddley" and extended his hand.

"I'm Marco – great name Diddley" said Marco as he extended his hand and the two shook hands fervently.

"What's your next class?" asked Diddley.

"Science. What about you?" answered Marco.

"Same" said Didd, "want to head over together?"

"Sure," said Marco, "I'll be glad to walk with Sir Diddley Squatt."

They both laughed and headed down the hallway; and thus began Diddley's newest friendship.

It only took a couple of days for Diddley and Marco to bond. Diddley learned that Marco was Italian and his family had come to America in the earlier 1900's Italian immigrant migration to America. Marco schooled Diddley how the Italian immigrants came to America seeking economic opportunities. They settled in many southern areas, some along the Mississippi Delta; some of the families settled along the Mississippi Gulf Coast in the Biloxi/Gulfport area, and others spread across the southern states of Arkansas. They found work where they could – some picked cotton in the cotton fields; some worked in canning and fishing industries; others were merchants, operating grocery stores, liquor stores, and tobacco shops.

"How come I've never seen Italians before I met you?" asked Diddley.

"I dunno - my family first sent me to an elementary school outside of Rundown City, but then my dad got laid-off, and now we are back in Rundown Schools," said Marco.

"Let me tell you a little about the history I heard from my dad and mom and grandparents," said Marco, "See, when the cotton field/farm work and other factory work starting drying up around this area – most of my ancestors and family moved up North and West. My family stayed down here; so here me and my brothers and sisters are. And believe me, black people aren't the only ones being unfairly treated. Me and my family? As one of the few Italian families left in the Rundown City area- we could tell you some stories about what the white folks felt about us and being treated unfairly because of being Italian and more brown-skinned and different - and "immigrants." That's why I'm glad I met you and could feel you would understand; being negro and darker than us. I'm glad to call you a new friend," said Marco.

"I feel and felt the same way when I first turned around and saw you in math class; we have stuff in common" laughed Diddley, "I just knew we would connect."

"What other stuff might we have in common?" asked Marco.

"'I'm told my dad's real first name was "Deangelo", but nobody remembers his last name, "answered Diddley.

"Oh my goodness!" said Marco excitedly, "I know for sure Deangelo is an Italian name. Your father could be part Italian?

"I know," said Didd, "that probably explains our instant bond. Plus - look at our hair and how similar yours is to mine. We may be Italano brothers my friend" said Didd as they both SCREAM and laugh out loud, grab each other around the neck, and playfully fall to the ground while hugging through chuckles of laughter.

Diddley and Marco quickly became great friends. Diddley was invited over and met all of Marco's brothers and sisters. He especially loved Marco's mother who everybody called "Mama Valentus" (similar to Diddley's Momma Squatt) because she always greeted Diddley with a hug and invited him in for suppers of this fantastic dish called "la-sag-na" and especially "spa-get-tti." He always put extra cheese on his when Mama Valentus plated his up. All of Marco's family would be seated around this huge table and Marco's mom would have this huge spread of food ready; Mama and Pop Valentus would be talking loud and telling stories, as the lasagna and spaghetti and meatballs and rolls and salad was passed around and enjoyed by all. Laughter... laughter... laughter all around.

Then one day. Would you believe it? Just as Diddley and Marco were bonding - Pop Valentus got a job in New York and the family uprooted quickly and moved. Unbelievable!!!

Diddley remembers his and Marco's last conversation they had in the woods behind the Copp-A-Squatt. They were sitting on some tree stumps, each with a bottle of root beer in their hand:

"Can't believe we are moving up north" said Marco.

"A lot of the folks in this area are doing the same," said Diddley" blacks and whites; everybody-that's where the opportunities are."

"Thank you for being my friend Diddley," said Marco, "You are going to make something of yourself. Although we barely got to know each other and just got it going, I know you are going to be successful and happy in life, because you have a good loving heart. My whole family told me to tell you and they all feel the same. I am willing to bet that one day we will run into each other again. We can then share another bottle of root beer."

"Marco Valentus – the same back to you and your family. Whenever I was at your house, your family made me feel like family. I never felt like a black outsider kid. You have taught me, as a few other non-negro kids I've befriended - that regardless of who you are; or what color you are; or what country you are from; or if you are immigrants; or if you are rich or poor - we are all the same if you just take the time to sit down and talk and listen to each other. You have taught me a lesson of love and understanding I will carry with me forever – love every human regardless of all else. And also… please tell your mom that she made this lesson easy to learn because she introduced me to and makes the best spaghetti and meatballs I've ever tasted!!"

They both laughed and clicked root-beer bottles. Marco and his family were gone the next day.

Those first few days/months of high school passed, Diddley thought how he loved education that was provided at all of his schools – not just school education but life stuff like friendship and how to carry yourself in the world. And now, especially at Rundown High, the learning process continued.

However, a different education continued at the Copp –A-Squatt –Inn (more on that later:) but he loved both equally.

At Rundown High, young Didd really dug into regular classes like math, science, and history. As mid-year first year came, Diddley often thought about his lost friends Pryor and Marco and what they would miss as being friends through high school. He often thought how in their brief friendships they would walk home from school, put on baseball gloves and play catch – or shoot basketball together; how they would walk and talk through the streets or the woods, and discuss similar rough spots in life and school they encountered. After Pryor was gone, Diddley felt Marco would be his next friend to share his life encounters; but now even that was gone. Diddley wondered if he was cursed and couldn't keep friendships?

Diddley, of course, moved on. He dug into school; found learning very interesting and loved reading about stuff he didn't know about like:

1.) Science - In science, he loved reading about the stars and the moon; the sky; nature of all aspects. Didd, of course, loved all animals and enjoyed reading about all animal habits, their lifestyle, their mating habits, etc. The idea that humans should do more to protect the earth, the skies, the oceans -like conservation of resources, re-cycling, and using more earth friendly products - this made perfect logical sense to Diddley.

2.) Math - Believe it or not, Diddley actually enjoyed reading and learning the who's/what's/whys of math and how the aspects of mathematics played in everything connected with life; percentages of how and why there were so many more poor black folks than poor white folks; why children who came from one family homes (the vast majority of kids living with their mother after their father split) were more mathematically pre-deposed to not make it in life and die an early life rather than those kids with a mom and dad raising them. He was even interested in gambling, and eventually learned why all the pimps and hustlers at the Copp-A-Squatt lost either all their money at the illegal gambling halls; or even when just playing cards in the foyer -the odds were stacked against you when gambling!

3.) History – Young Didd loved reading about history. It came simply to him and seemed so obvious – how could one know how to go forward or better himself in life if he didn't know about the history of the things of the past? It seemed easy to figure out this applied not only to each living individual, but also to society as a whole. So, he learned not only about George Washington and Abraham Lincoln and the Constitution, but also about Dredd Scott and Harriet

Tubman, as well as Frederick Douglas, the fighter Jack Johnson and track star Jessie Owens - all the early black heroes. As he was getting into his teens, he also more keenly observed, without anybody telling him, that Rundown was primarily a black school district; and he'd have to be sure to stay on top of his academics. He'd lay awake at night with his light on in his cramped room, falling asleep with a book on his chest, until Chastity or Momma Squatt would come in and remove the book and tuck him into bed.

4.) Sports education at school: Diddley was an excellent athlete. He first noticed his physical transformation around the ages of 11 and 12 years of age. He had natural sports instincts and made any football, baseball, basketball, and tracks teams he went out for - a great athlete! He was without doubt the best male athlete during his Rundown Elementary/Middle School years, and picked right up as he starred on the freshman and first year football and basketball teams beginning at Rundown High. He led his team in rushing in freshman football; played guard and forward on the basketball teams; pitched, played a flawless 3rd base, and hit over 400 in every season of baseball. Track? Diddley won the city championship in the 200 meters. It all came natural to Diddley, so athletics really wasn't the *turn on* for Young Didd. He felt the need for other challenges.

5.) Girl Education – Didd had gotten used to the bullying years at Rundown Elementary/Middle School – and as he eased into his high school years the bullying no longer bothered him, and eased his mind as he only had a few isolated incidences in high school. Kids no longer even bothered him about living at the Copp-A-Squatt. As a matter of fact, young guys would come up to him and ask about what went on and to relay stories about the girls and even if he had seen some of the girls naked, etc? Didd just laughed, and he knew he would never give details about his loved ones at the Copp-A-Squatt... NEVER. And his curly hair? As he moved on, the girls gave him compliments instead of insults as he grew more and more handsome by the day. Things were definitely on the upswing for young Didd.

Girls? Instead of sneering and insulting him, they now noticed and complimented him as they passed by in the halls of Rundown High School. Here's a taste of the scene:

Girls: *"Diddley the squiddley... let's find out if you can truly diddle Diddley?"*

Girls: *"Diddley Doo right... you can doo me – right?"*

Girls: *"Let's see if you can really squat... you Diddley Squatt you!"*

Girls: *"You can diddle my fiddle..."*

What a change!

One girl did catch Didd's eye thou.

Something was different about her in Didd's eyes. Her name was Glorendous Zoowalter, and the first time Diddley saw her he thought she was the most beautiful girl he had ever seen. Strange name maybe (maybe because she had a strange name like him- that was the immediate attraction?) but Glorendous was this very chocolate-colored girl with enormous eyes, beautiful eyes... green emerald eyes; the whitest teeth ever; thin but not too thin - eyes, skin, smile that just burned through your skin when she looked directly at you. She had

47

this long kinky hair that cascaded down from both sides of her face, like waterfalls. And she wore this African type of clothing called "dashiki" or something like that – absolutely beautiful black girl!

Young Diddley couldn't quite understand why he was so attracted to her? She didn't say a word, a peep, to Diddley or anybody else. He would pass her in the hallways or on the athletic fields during gym, and she rarely looked his way. However, you can bet he was always looking her way, just hoping to get a return glance.

One day after football practice, as Didd was leaving the field – he saw Glorendous finishing a sprint around the track – she must have been a track athlete practicing. When she crossed the finish line, Didd ran up to her.

"Wow… you are some athlete" he said sheepishly.

She shyly looked his way and said "Not really, I just do it to keep the parts moving. My dad always said people from my country like to move to keep the heart running and in good order. It's Ok but I could really do without it."

"My name is Diddley - and I think you are the most beautiful human being God ever created," Didd said.

Immediately, he stopped- caught his breath - and couldn't believe what he just said.

"I don't know what to say" said Glorendous with a shy smile," I know who you are Diddley Squatt. I know about all the bullying and name calling; and where you live, and now I feel ashamed that I didn't come to your aid and offer help when all the bulling was going on. Why on earth would you even look my way or talk to me? I never helped you," said Glorendous.

"None of that matters; we can only go forward," said Diddley.

"I have no idea how you took all that wicked bullying. In the country I come from, the elders would have never accepted such a thing." she said.

"Oh… and where are you from?" asked Diddley as the two moved toward the broken-down gym at Rundown High.

"My family is originally from Cameroon – a country in Central Africa. Before I was born my dad hitched a ride from Africa to America to work in the fields and coal mines with hopes of making a better life for himself. Once here, he met a young girl and fell in love and they soon married and starting working in the fields and various coal mines in the states here and there; all in hopes to make a good living and life for a family they started. Soon came me and my brothers and sisters; the mine and factory jobs tanked- so we moved to Rundown and my mom and dad have been working hard ever since.

"Sigh – I know your story," said Didd, "I've heard the same from many of the students here on how they landed in Rundown."

They reached the gym.

"Well Glorendous, it has been so nice finally meeting you and talking to you. I must say once again – you are the most beautiful girl I've ever seen and I hope we can talk in the future."

"Sounds good to me young Diddley" said Glorendous as she waded into the girl's gym.

Over the next few weeks Diddley and Glorendous talked every day between classes; at lunch, after school as he walked her home. A couple of times they even held hands as they strolled toward home.

Then, on a day that Diddley will never forget, as they near Glorendous's small frame house - Didd notices a "FOR SALE" sign in the shabby front lawn.

Glorendous then breaks into uncontrollable tears; just crying madly.

"What's wrong? Did something happen? Is your family really moving? I'm deeply sorry," said Diddley.

"You did nothing wrong," said Glorendous," it's just that although our high school years just started, my dad told us yesterday that he got a new/better job back in Cameroon and we will be moving soon -back to Cameroon. Can you believe it? You finally decide to talk to me, and I to you, and I was becoming comfortable with a boy for the first time in my life - and this may be the last few times we may be together.

Didd stood their holding their school books, stunned at the news. Here he finally got the up the nerve to talk to a girl. She liked him too, and things were going great... but now she was leaving? Didd thought to himself "am I a born loser?"

His mind started racing. What was it with him and friends who he truly got close to - that they would all leave? First Pryor Richards; then Marco Valentus; and now the one girl out of the 3 – Glorendous, was also leaving? He thought he must be cursed!!!!!!

"Glorendous, I can't believe this is happening this way. I finally meet a girl and garner the nerve to talk to her; and you are in a similar situation and gather the nerve to respond to me. And now we learn that it was all in vain?"

Diddley looks toward the sky.

"Dear God... maybe I am jinxed by my name! I can't keep a good friend - maybe Diddley ain't Squatt!!!"

Didd stood there looking into the heavens; couldn't move... can you believe it? About to ask the first girl in his life if maybe she would be his first girlfriend ever -and she was moving?

Glorendous could see that Diddley was badly hurt and shocked by this news. She moved in close to him and said through tears:

"You are special young Diddley Squatt. God does things for a purpose. I don't know what to say." She stopped and took Diddley's hand; they were hunkered under this old decrepit spruce tree and it was late, close to dark.

"Diddley, you are one special human being. You are going to do great things – I FEEL IT – I hope I do great things when I go back to Cameroon and learn the culture. However, I do have feelings for you and will carry those feelings with me across the ocean. Please, please, give me my first and last kiss here in America; if you think I am worthy?"

Didd moved close to Glorendous.

"Glorendous, you have no idea how much I feel for you, and like my luck, it ends before it even begins. However, I've quickly learned that it is what it is. You are indeed my first girlfriend – if only for a night."

Diddley then takes Glorendous in his arms and their lips tell the story. They kiss long and tender... long and tender... long and tender...

A warm and passionate kiss that lasts at least a minute.

They unleash. Glorendous moves homeward toward her front door while the last tears fall from her beautiful green eyes. She gets to the front door and waves at Diddley. She then disappears into the house.

They see each other one last time, and then Glorendous is gone. Gone before it even started.

While his first romantic experience may have ended with just his first kiss - but didn't go any further - at least Diddley got his first kiss - and it was such a lovely kiss!

Sigh… life moves on quickly. As luck would have it, and about a month after his Glorendous first kiss affair, Didd ran right into another man/woman experience from an unexpected source that at least shed some further life on this "birds and bees" stuff. Remember now, Didd didn't have a dad or uncle to explain this man woman stuff to him. Yes, he had kissed his first girl Glorendous, but that was just a one-night insight stuff. Didd's next "educational experience" after Glorendous, and who provided it, added immensely to his first years of high school and the learning there. He felt he deserved some type of break after losing so many close friends as they moved out of Rundown.

Diddley was always adored by all the girls at Copp-A-Squatt, and as he continued to grow into a strapping young teen toward his adult-hood, all the other girls at the Copp-A-Squatt – in addition to some of the older girls at Rundown High, noticed him. The athletics, the heavy chores around the Inn with the lifting, moving of furniture up and down the stairs, all added to his maturing physique. Diddley was already muscular and graceful at 14.

The johns called Diddley when their cars needed a push, a jump, or just help getting the old rusted heap off the road. Anything anybody in the area had a need-for-help or a problem with, the first person they called for? You guessed it – the call went out. "Go get Diddley – he'll help." If someone then asked "Go get who?" the answer quickly became, "YOU DON'T KNOW DIDDLEY?"

One night, Young Didd was in his bedroom, a small, closet-like room that was situated next to the basement where Momma stored the illegal bootleg liquor and other food supplies from her under-the-table deals. Didd's room had a bed, a drawer, and one small window near the top of the ceiling that Didd had to stand on a chair to look out into the backyard. On the walls were pictures that Diddley diddled, as well as pictures of musicians he'd pulled from magazines in the Copp-A-Squatt foyer. Old musicians like King Biscuit, his friend Robert "Bobby" Johnson, Wolf–A-Howlin, Sun House, Hooker John, Parker Bird, Many Miles, Charlie Stinky Black Muddy Water - you know, musicians of the day. Didd loved his room- it was all he needed.

Diddley was in his room preparing for bed. Before shutting his eyes to the world completely for the night, Didd always went to the bathroom first so he could have a good night's sleep. Since there was no bathroom in the basement, Didd ran up the stairs to use one of the common bathrooms on one of the upper floors of the Copp-A-Squatt. Each bathroom had a couple of urinals; a couple of creaky wooden closeted toilets for privacy; and finally, a shower space made up of a couple of old leaky showers hanging from the wall/ceiling area where folks could rinse off. Sinks hung to the left wall with mirrors over them for the johns/renters to shave. Not much, but it was workable.

Diddley was making his nightly bathroom run, standing over the urinal and peeing, when old Rusty Bhutt (that's what they called him) walked in and used the urinal right next to Diddley. Rusty was the oldest Copp-A-Squatt resident, a bit wobbly, and considered by all to be on his last legs. Momma let him keep a room because he tended to the garden and, more importantly, he was a bootleg tester extraordinaire. The man could tell the good hooch from the real rotgut with just one whiff and sip.

Rusty peered over at Young Didd peeing, and says: "Hey young buck, you ever use that thing you holding on a girl?"

Didd was taken aback by the question, but answered while still concentrating on the task at hand:

"Are you referring to sex? I've heard both the johns and women talk about sex, so yeah, I know what it is. But I'm a little young, don't you think, Rusty?"

Rusty burst out laughing. "Yeah. Sex with a woman... doing the nasty... whatever you want to call it; and with a woman. You wouldn't have sex with a man, would you? They call them types of people sissies and queers." Rusty gave him a hard look. "You ain't queer, are you, young stuff?" Rusty coughed out a gravelly laugh.

"No, I'm not queer, but I don't judge people even if they were "queer" as you say. Who am I to judge somebody? In those Sunday School Classes Momma Squatt and the girls take me to, we learn than only Jesus Christ and God can judge us."

"So now you going to church on me, huh? You brought it up, but you don't think it's wrong if some boys only like boys and maybe some girls only like girls?" Rusty says as he splishes and splashes, but waits patiently for Didd's reply.

"Not for me to judge'" says Diddly firmly, "God put all us humans and animals here on earth for a purpose. People can't help who they are. I get teased because my name is Diddley, when I had absolutely nothing to do with it. People have the right to be who they are. You ever think maybe they didn't even have a choice if they were born "queer" as you say."

"Ha! Well, at least you answerin' the questions truthfully, young buck." Rusty Bhutt smiles wide and slaps the wall in amazement with Didd's response.

"I've been called sissy, and other names, just because of my name, so I know how people feel for stuff they have no control over. The Bible says "love thy neighbor," and not "love only thy neighbor who only likes the other sex" – so that's what I try to live by. It works for me," said Diddley confidently.

"You like puppies Mr. Rusty?" Didd then asks.

"Do I like puppies?" says Rusty with a look of amazement. "What the hell do puppies have to do with sex and queers and sissies?"

"Be at a park, or at a barbeque at Momma Squatt's back yard, and watch what happens when somebody brings a puppy. That puppy runs up to each and every person who reaches down to pet him. That puppy doesn't care if you are black or white, fat or skinny, male or female, sissy or queer, young or old. It doesn't care if your name is Rusty Bhutt or Diddley Squatt. That puppy doesn't judge anybody because he doesn't care or may not even know you, all he sees are your friendly hands reaching out to welcome and pet him. If you pet him, you have a friend for life!"

"Damn! You are a smart little sucker ain't you?" Rusty breaks out into another round of laughter. "I gotta give you that. Thanks for the lesson. But let's get back to my first question. Have you ever had any sex? I had my first girl at age 12 and I know you can take it boy. Plus – you live at the best place in the world to get your first "sexual encounter" if you prefer to say it that way. You don't have to answer me now; but I know I've put something on that young mid of yours" Rusty said as he finished up – washed his hands – and left the bathroom

Diddley finished at the urinal, and moved to the sink to wash his hands. He was still a little stunned at Rusty's initial question. He had let Rusty know that he knew about some worldly stuff, and that was good… but how much did he really want to divulge to this Rusty dude. Didd gave his face a good hard look in the mirror, and thought to himself as he continued to look at his face in the mirror.

"Am I ready to try some sex?' he thought to himself. "I mean, that's what the Copp-A-Squatt was about anyway, right?" He had never even thought about it until this moment.

Now, from this unexpected source of Rusty Bhutt, the idea of sex was definitely on his mind.

CHAPTER 5

Diddley Becomes Fascinated with Music

Remember, Didd had been surrounded with music since he was a little child. Nate the Skate's harmonica lessons, the "gitar/geetar" that GG Prince first introduced to him, all the music coming from the rooms, all the noisy weekends. It was that "geetar" that always pulled at him, the one that really spoke to him in his heart. GG let him pick his from time to time, but he never had one of his own. Something spoke to him on the inside and he got the feeling he needed to start taking the guitar more seriously… it was just a gut feeling.

Here's the story of how he fell in love with music and the guitar:

DIDDLEY LEARNS TO PLAY THE GUITAR:

During those early years of Didd's life, a frequent visitor to the bordello was an old blues guitar player named Bobby Johnson. His real name was Robert Johnson, but everybody just called him Bobby. Like a lot of Momma Squatt's customers,

Bobby took an immediate fancy to Diddley, and began teaching him some simple guitar chords. He showed him the basic chords, nothing fancy. C chord, D chord, E chord; basic blues chords, basic stuff. Didd picked it up immediately, which didn't surprise Bobby because he had heard Diddley doodling on the harmonica and knew he had some musical talent inside there.

"Young man," said Bobby one day, "I am going to tell you something very important and gift you at the same time. Take this notebook, it is called a journal. Write in this journal as often as you can. Doesn't matter if it is guitar notes, questions and answers to Chastity or Momma Squatt, your daily thoughts - just write down your thoughts as often as you can. I think one day you will want to write songs, and your daily thoughts will help you with the lyrics and stories. This is some of the best advice I can give a young cat." Didd took the ruffled journal and held onto it tightly.

Bobby Johnson was in his 80's at this time, and he knew the end was nearing. During the stretch while he got to know Didd, watching him grow day by day, Bobby looked into his young protégé's eyes, knowing that with his last days approaching, he had to pass on all his gifts, both his worldly ideas as well as his guitar playing expertise. When he looked into Diddley's eyes, he knew Diddley was indeed a sacred soul!

So, to recap, Diddley, now in the 10th grade and 15 years-old, was no longer bullied because the word got around the small town quickly about the Herbert Hebert situation. He never left home without the pocket harmonica Nate the Skate had given to him. Now he also has his journal stuffed in his back pocket; two very important life lessons and possessions for young Diddley Squatt.

Right when Diddley was getting into learning both the harmonica and, more recently, the guitar, Nate the Skate was found sick and vomiting in one of Momma Squatt's rooms, and died a few days later. The police thought maybe Nate was fooling around not only with a Momma Squatt girl – but maybe also with a married woman on the outside, and maybe the married woman's husband somehow poisoned Nate. Things like this happened all the time in Rundown City – and since it happened at the Copp- A-Squatt-Inn and in the black neighborhood- the cops didn't investigate or care that much. To them, it was just one less nigger (dead) they had to deal with. Sigh…

Bobby's very regular weekends forays into the Copp-A-Squatt to visit and partake of Chastity or the other girls, always ended with him at least stopping by and showing Diddley some new guitar tricks/licks. Bobby would show Diddley guitar chords and talk about how the guitar was a sacred instrument and how once one learned to play just basic chords and licks, he could "talk to the gods." The guitar was indeed a magical instrument.

Bobby Johnson and Diddley established a unique bond. Didd also remembered some of the ladies saying that Bobby was a "stud" even at 80. The girls said he was legendary for how long he could last in the bedroom (whatever that meant – ''That old dude is something else," he heard the girls say," My goodness, Bobby would want to go at it all night.")

Robert always dressed sharp. It didn't matter if it was night or day, he always, always, wore sunglasses. Man, those were some nice-looking sunglasses! Anyway, Didd remembered Bobby telling him:

"Young Didd, you are too young to know what this means – but God gifted me with an enormous and powerful 3rd leg. When you get older, ask the old folks what that means." Bobby chuckled. "One day soon you will know what I'm talking about, young stud."

Time passed, and one-day Didd heard some sad news. His good friend Chastity whispered to him that Robert "Bobby" Johnson was dying from something mysterious called "cancer." Back in those days, folks just died and never knew what they might be dying from; they were just dying. This cancer thing was new, but it was scary.

Chastity said people were talking, that rumors were that Bobby was poisoned maybe like Nate the Skate; maybe he too had charmed the wrong girl, and her boyfriend had looked for revenge. Rumors like this were nothing new.

Robert Johnson was in Room 32 of the Copp-A-Squatt, casually dying. Robert's room was always filled with the midwives, the nurses, and Rundown's one "doctor" who everybody called Doctor Feelgood. His real name was DaRock Feelgut M.D. but everybody soon shortened the name and he was forever known as "Dr. Feelgood" This came about because one year this up and coming singer named Aretha passed through Rundown and felt rundown – so she called the good Doc and he helped her and she claimed "one year I'm going to name a song after you." Bobby was dying, and folks from near and far came to Room 32 and paid their respects to the man who had played so many blues jams for them. Soooooo many blues clubs; so many blues songs for everybody, often for free, but always with the joy of just spreading his music. Bobby always enjoyed himself so much, even playing for just pennies. All for the love of the music.

Diddley found himself amongst the crowd in Room 32. The pimps, the whores, the musicians, even white folks paying their last respects.

"No telling how much longer Robert has," Dr. Feelgood told the throng," but it won't be long until Robert is singing and slinging with the angels."

The next day, Didd was walking past Room 32 and looked in, afraid because he thought Robert would be dead. He hadn't ever seen a dead person before. He was surprised when he heard the raspy voice coming from the bed.

"Young Didd, come in. I've been waiting for you."

Didd walked in and stood over Robert. Robert's face was wrinkled, with deep unshaven valleys and crevices. For the first time he can remember, Robert removed his signature sunglasses to reveal his normally brown eyes. They were steady; and had a grayish film formed over them. He looked deep into Diddley's eyes.

"Boy, you have something special in you, I can see it in your eyes. You have an old soul, and I know you are destined to do great things." Robert winced a bit. "Don't be afraid. You and I are kindred souls. That means we were meant to be friends by God." Bobby took a deep breath and settled back.

"I like the sound of those words," kindred souls," said Diddley loudly. "They sound like soothing words." Didd took out his trusty journal and jotted down the words "kindred souls."

Robert spoke again: "You have a great and giving soul, and one of your talents is music. You are definitely a musical artist. Hell, you might even be a writer or a Renaissance man of many talents, singer, musician, painter, sculptor, writer, poet, and actor, or something else, but you have God given talent that MUST be explored. So, I want to help you. I want to take you to a special place, but I don't know if this old body or my circumstances will allow me to take you to this special place I need to tell you about. I need to take you!"

Didd stood there looking into Bobby's eyes and he indeed felt something special happening to him. For really the first time in his life, he knew that somebody, especially <u>an adult</u>, was trying to tell him something that was *real* and the *truth*. He could feel it! He took Robert's words to heart and he blurted out, "Bobby, I have something special I can do that I've never shared with anyone – not anyone. If you really think we are "kindred souls" and you think it is important to show me something somewhere, I think I can get us there."

"I knew it!" said Bobby through a horrid cough. He turned and spit into a bucket on the floor. His eyes widened and he pulled his head up from the couch, as excited as Didd had ever seen him. "We are indeed kindred souls. Now tell me, how can we get where I need to get you before our gracious God takes me to the other side?"

"Well, I've got two special powers that will get us there, and we don't need anybody else or a car, mules, wagon - anything. You just have to have faith in me and believe I can do it," said Didd quietly.

"Shit. Faith is all I got left, young Didd!" Robert wheezed and coughed. "Let's do it!"

"I'll come get you at midnight, after I'm supposed to be in bed," said Young Didd.

"Ok with me… but how we going?" asked a perplexed Robert.

"Don't worry – just be ready and be sure to have on some sturdy shoes and a very, very warm overcoat," said Diddley as he left the room. "Just be ready." Robert laid there with not a word or idea in his head; but he still found himself as excited as he'd ever been in his life.

Robert was weakening, but the smile on his face matched the glint in his eye.

CHAPTER 6

Two Kindred Souls Unite
at the Crossroads

That night, at 12 midnight, young Didd crept into Robert's room without making a sound. Didd was wearing his favorite overalls for comfort. Robert noticed he had that ever-present little harmonica on a chain around his neck. He also had something bulging in his front overall pocket.

"Where's the help?" said Robert as he slowly pulled himself upright to sit on the bed. He had on his favorite white shirt and old suit jacket with a nice, warm overcoat over it all buttoned to the top, and indeed some black-and-white Stacey Adams shoes, of course all spit-shined. And yes, he had on his ever-present sunglasses. Robert was cool as ice water!

"We have all the help we need right here," Diddley pulled out an old empty honey jar, with the top screwed on it but holes poked in the top for air, out of his overalls front pocket. Robert looked in closely, and could barely see the tiny ladybug with red wings and black spots flying around in the jar.

"Young Didd – what the hell is that?" said an exasperated Robert.

"You said you had faith in me, my kindred soul friend. Just hold on and don't be afraid," said Diddley as he placed the jar on the bed next to Robert and pulled his magic harmonica to his lips with his left hand. "Hold my hand and close your eyes. Don't open them until I tell you to. Also, please don't yell out to wake anyone. We will be on our way in a few seconds." Diddley then played the first bars of "I Put a Spell on You" to warm up his blowing chops, and was well into the second stanza when he hit hole number **one** on his harmonica - the LOWEST note on the harmonica. It took some extra playing because there were two people involved instead of Didd alone.

> *Robert could feel the room start to spin as a funny sensation took over his body. He felt like he was floating above the bed and spinning at the same time. "What the hell have I let this boy do?" he said to himself; but true to his word, he didn't open his eyes. This sensation went on for about a minute. Then, he felt some warm covers engulfing his body. He assumed Diddley had thrown some blankets over him. He couldn't feel his feet touching the floor. "Okay… you can open your eyes now" said Didd. When Robert opened his eyes – he thought he was dreaming. He was indeed engulfed in covers-the bed covers- and as he removed the covers from his face - the first place he looked was up high and noticed the ceiling was WAY… WAY… UP HIGH? He looked to his right, and there was Diddley sitting next to him. When he looked to his left, to his amazement, was the ladybug, a shade bigger than him? He looked into her beautiful huge eyes, and she looked back at him, tilted her head, and batted her beautiful huge eyelashes. she appeared to smile into his frozen face.*

"What is this? Is this a dream?" Was all he could say.

"Not a dream" said Diddley, "I just made you small like me and my friend the ladybug. That's one of the powers I discovered I had. I played "I Put a Spell on You" on my harp; blew just the right run, and then this magic happens," said Diddley proudly. As Robert tried to decide if this was weird or a strange dream, he moved to the end of the bed and looked over. The floor seemed a mile away. He scrambled to Young Didd and said," What about the Ladybug – is she going to eat us?"

Diddley and LadyM laughed hardily.

" No way. Mr. Robert Johnson, I present to you my ladybug friend, Mademoiselle LadyM. She's my good friend and very nice. She's our ride to wherever you said you wanted to take me. What do you think of THAT?"

"Hello, Robert. Nice to meet you," said LadyM as she flapped her wings and batted those nice eyelashes.

Robert was so shocked all he could do was sit there and try to take it all in. He looked around, wide eyed. All the pictures in Room 32 were 5 times as large. The dresser, the mirror, everything looked like giants. Robert swallowed hard.

"I'm no bigger than an ant... that's why I felt those covers."

"You OK?" said Diddley to Robert, "we best be on our way." When Diddley stood, LadyM moseyed up to him and squatted down on her legs so Diddley could climb on her back. He wrapped his harmonica chain around her neck carefully so he and Robert would have something to hold onto. "Hop on" he told Robert.

Robert was shaking, but finally able to stand on his weakened legs, and Didd grabbed his hand and pulled him on LadyM's back.

"It's like sitting on an old mule, Robert, but LadyM is much softer. Now hold on tight, YIPPIE KYE AAAAAAAAA!" he yelled as LadyM easily lifted them into the air.

"Let's ease around the room a bit until your friend gets his sea legs —or in this case - his air legs" said LadyM. Up in the air they twirled, as LadyM started circling the room, past the dresser, the mirror, the pictures. Robert at first didn't open his eyes, but as he felt the wind against his face, he finally opened them and could see they were indeed buzzing around the room. Soon Robert relaxed, and seemed to enjoy the sensation. Robert quickly calmed down from the shock with the realization that this was real.

LadyM asked, "So, where to?"

"My exact question?" asked Didd, "Where is this special place we must see?"

"Clarksdale, Mississippi," said Robert Johnson.

"Clarksdale, Mississippi?" said Diddley, "I never heard of it."

"I have," said LadyM, "I know it well. Pretty long ride. I will have to use my special jet-speed powers to get us there in a timely manner. Let's get on our journey my human friends.'"

With that LadyM took one last twirl around Room 32, and headed out the door, down the stairs past the late-night drunks and girls in the stairwell who didn't even notice a ladybug with two miniaturized humans on her back. Down past the smoke filled Copp –A-Squatt main lobby where johns were busy playing tonk, bid-whist, and poker, where the girls draped themselves on dude's shoulders, sat on laps drinking whiskey, and flirted; skirts and thighs shooting into the air. They flew past the kitchen where LadyM, Didd, and Robert could smell the ever-present fried chicken and greens and turnips simmering on the stove, and then they hit the open back door and… "ZOOOOOM" were soon out into the darkness of night. LadyM's wings fluttered furiously and made a wistful, yet safe sounding buzz, like a small engine.

Soon, Diddley and Robert Johnson were hanging on for dear life as LadyM had really cut loose with her ladybug special speed motors! The young lady was no slouch. Unlike regular ladybugs, LadyM had some juice in the goose and in those powerful wings! They were easily moving at over 100 miles an hour. They were dipping in and out.

Diddley felt the gentle sway of Lady M, and with the vibrations of her wings felt words take shape in his mind…

"Past trees and tree branches
Over ponds and horse ranches

Soaring high and dipping low
Skirting mountains and lakes with blue flow

Dark of darkness with only stars for light
Sounds of nothing but sounds of night life

Howls of wolves and screams of owls
Us holding tight with windswept jowls

Dizzy and mind blowing; yet clear and fun
LadyM, me and Robert – what a run!

It seemed like they were flying for hours when LadyM finally said, "Coming up to Clarksdale, Mississippi soon, my friends. Should be about 10 minutes away. I must warn you that I'm a bit tired, but hopefully we will have a smooth landing. This has been quite the ride."

Didd and Robert were very excited looking down at the countryside. Soon, Robert shouted:

"Look… the graveyard!' pointing down to the right.

They looked to the right and there it was, the gravestones and grave-markers sticking out as if reaching to the sky; like toothpicks sticking out of the brown and green gravy yard.

"Clarksdale, Mississippi coming up in 5 minutes. All passengers prepare for landing," came LadyM's instructions. "Any specific location?"

"Right there. The Clarksdale Graveyard" said Robert through chattering teeth.

Graveyard? Young Didd's heart almost stopped beating. The questions ran through his head. Why in the world would Robert have Didd reveal his smalling and flying secrets, only to have him fly to a graveyard way out in the middle of nowhere deep in "Keep-Running" Mississippi? What could he learn from this experience? What lesson could he learn from a graveyard?

"Hope I haven't made a mistake" Diddley said to himself.

"Here we go00000000," said LadyM as we started our descent thru the bushes and trees.

"BOOM!"

Diddley could feel LadyM's legs starting to drop from her body – like landing gear dropping from the bottom of a plane he had seen in a book from school. Her legs fully extended downward, and suddenly, we stopped over the top of a grave and hovered like a helicopter. As LadyM's wings fluttered maddingly, a calmness settled over us. Soon, we were indeed on top of the marker and LadyM's engine shut down.

"Crew… prepare to depart," said LadyM. They had touched down on the top of a smooth, slick grave marker, laid flat amid the grass. We unbuckled from our tethers and each took steps down off LadyM and took our first steps down in Clarksdale, Mississippi.

Diddley and Robert found themselves sitting dead center in an enormous graveyard; markers and graves to the north, south, east and west. A huge sign smack in the middle of the graveyard shone with the bright neon lights proclaiming:

"WELCOME TO CLARKSDALE
MISSISSIPPI MUNICIPAL GRAVEYARD
(CMMG)"

LadyM fluttered those tremendous eyelashes of hers and sighed.

"Ok, boys. I got you here but I am very, very tired from the flight. I will need at least a couple hours sleep before we even think about heading back. I haven't flown such a distance in a while. I saw a pond a little way back where I can refresh myself with some green grass, and shrubs, and fresh-water. I'll find a safe lily pad to sleep on and come back refreshed. You men take care of your business, and after resting I will return and we can get back on the road home. Young Didd, I suggest you two discuss your business and "grow up" (chuckle) if you know what I mean."

LadyM took a couple of steps, then dropped her body low to take off mode, and was soon airborne, giving Didd and Robert a wink as she passed.

"OK Robert, lets first get tall and regular again," said Diddley.

"Yeah. Surprise me. How we gonna do that!" said an exhausted Robert.

"Easy. Let me do all the work," said Young Didd. He pursed his lips around his miniature harmonica and played the high # 10 hole on his harmonica <u>like mad.</u> Boom. Like magic, Diddley and Robert were soon their natural heights. Diddley took Robert's elbow and let him lean heavily on him.

"Man. I thought I knew about music. Wish I had gotten me one of those harmonicas!" said Robert. Didd had the next question.

"OK Robert. I've done my job and got us here. Now you gotta tell me why we are in a Mississippi graveyard at midnight."

"Only fair. My turn, my friend." Robert rested his cane on the side of a tree stump and took a seat. The air was so clear and brisk, the stars were as bright as city lights; it was a *magnificent night.* Diddley took a seat on the green grass.

"We are here because it is fate," he finally said, "young Diddley Squatt – you should now realize that without question you are special and were dropped on God's green earth for a special purpose. I know it, and a few other smart folks know it. But as is the usual case with most special folks, the special folks themselves don't know it! So, it is up to somebody to tell you.

I'm about at the end of my days, so I wanted to do this last good deed before I join my maker, hopefully in heaven. So, baby boy, let me tell you why we are here on this particular spot on this special beautiful night.

Diddley, we are here to undo something that I did years ago, to hopefully straighten it out and I can come to some type of understanding, and then bless you with certain "other" powers as you move through your life. You've already shown me you are blessed, but hopefully I can leave you with something to help you even more in your life.

"Huh?" said Diddley. Robert laughed, picked up his cane, righted himself, and wrapped his arm around Diddley's shoulders as they began strolling through the graveyard.

Robert then begins his story:

"Long ago when I was a young boy; a little older than you are now, all I wanted to be in life was a great musician, a great guitarist. I wanted to make something out of myself. I didn't want to have to work in the fields, or a factory, or a coal mine. I wanted to do something exciting. One hot, simmering day, I'm sitting on our porch in Clarksdale strumming this old piece of plywood with strings I fashioned from fishing wire, my attempt at a guitar, when this guy happened by. He said his name was Sun. Sun House. Anyway, he said it was amazing I was even getting a tune from my self-made guitar. He pulled out a harmonica, and I played the strings on my homemade guitar as Sun played along with his crazy harmonica. Afterward, he said he was also a guitar player but he also always carried his trusty harmonica with him for occasions such as this. After seeing your exploits on the harmonica, I'm sad I didn't add the harmonica to my repertoire of instruments. But, back to the story…

"You wanna learn how to play guitar?"' Sun asked me.

"Sure?"' I said. I jumped at the chance.

"Meet me at the Crossroads at midnight tonight,"' said Sun.

"'What's the Crossroads?"' I said.

"The white folks know it as the Clarksdale Mississippi Municipal Cemetery, but all the black folk know it as the Crossroads. For some reason," laughed Sun House. "'Come alone to the middle of the Crossroads."

Now little Didd, you have to know I was scared shitless about coming to a cemetery at midnight. However, I wanted to learn to play the guitar, and I desperately wanted to get out of Clarksdale and visit the rest of this round world. Shit. I would have gone to the moon if it meant getting out of Clarksdale and Mississippi. Just like the way I'm sure you feel – although it is a pretty good city… you feel about one day getting out of Rundown City and seeing more of this different world," croaked Robert.

"So, come midnight I made my way to the Crossroads and it is pitch black except for this big ass white moon shining down. The moon's rays glancing off the marble headstones were the only light. I made my way to the center of this scary place; nothing moving and no sounds except for the howls of coyotes and dogs. I'm looking around, waiting for Sun to appear, when all of sudden I see what looks like a shadow coming straight at me. The shadow is covered in this hood from head-to-toe, just floating, hovering, coming straight to me. I am so terrified -but at the same time thrilled, you know?

The shadow stopped in front of me and I all I could see was blackness in the hood, No face.

"Who are you?" A deep voice boomed from the hood.

"I'm Bobby Johnson," I said, "this guitar player named Sun House told me to meet him here and he'd work some kind of magic and I'd learn to play the guitar. Sun ain't here yet, but I'm sure he will be here soon."

"He's not coming, but we can commence with business. My name is Mr. DeVile," said the shadow with confidence.

"So, what happens next?" I said.

"It's simple," said the Mr. DeVile, "You turn over all your good thoughts about doing good in this world. Any thoughts about worshipping this guy called God, and I will give you special powers to play your stringed instrument and you will have the wishes you want about leaving Mississippi and traveling the world; playing your songs and meeting and sleeping with many women in this world, the primary goal a man, really wants. Lust. Freedom. Sin. Women. What else could a poor man want? Just turn your soul over to me."

Well, I thought, that sounded like a very good bargain.

"Where do I sign?"

"No signing needed," said the hooded figure, "Just say the word and your soul is mine."

Well, I figured, what did I need a soul for, anyway?

"OK, take it – it's yours," I said.

Robert stopped talking and choked up, coughing. He dropped to his knees thinking about his past.

"That's it, Robert?' asked Diddley, completely confused. "That's all?"

When Robert had composed himself, he looked in Diddley's eyes and said "You don't understand. It's simple. Mr. DeVile was actually the **DEVIL!!!!** I sold my soul to the devil for what I thought would be all the riches here on earth. But now as I near the end of my life I realize what a mistake I made," Robert trembled as he spoke.

"But you got your wish. You left Clarksdale and traveled the world playing your music, you became famous and made money, saw the world, had all the manly pleasures, I'm sure, and then came back south and to Rundown City to live the rest of your life in peace and quiet at Momma Squatt's. What's bad about that?" said Diddley.

"You don't understand," said Robert. "I cheated! I did it all the wrong way And I don't want that to happen to you. Young Didd, I am indeed living my last days on this good earth; but I never liked the way I got my talent. I haven't had a peaceful night's sleep in a good 50 years. I need to pass along to someone what I experienced so that I can leave this earth with peace on my mind, with a clear conscience that the devil and others can't touch. Please listen to me," Robert grabbed Didd by the shoulders and spoke directly into his eyes.

"Never, Never, EVER sellout your feelings or your true beliefs for any short-cuts in life.

Falseness will smack you in the face. You must earn your talent. <u>Study and practice your guitar – or your studies if you choose; just know there is no short magical way to succeed in life.</u> And please say your prayers at night to our almighty God. God is our friend and will watch your back. If you have the genius in you that I think you do, let go and let God."

Diddley saw Robert's eyes blazing in the moonlight.

"I hear you, Robert. So then, Mr. DeVile isn't coming here tonight, is he?" He could feel the hairs stand up on his neck.

"I doubt it, but you never know," said Robert as he got up from his knees, "but you just never know. Our crazy asses are smack dab in the middle of a graveyard at a strange hour; who knows. I only had that one encounter with Mr. DeVile, a.k.a. the devil, and I've never heard from him since."

"Then again, every night while I was on that bandstand playing my guitar for the folks in the audience, my heart was never clear. I've never killed anybody nor did anything terrible, but I gave up my faith in the Lord that night at the Crossroads. That was bad enough. Now I'm hoping for a little redemption by bringing you here and hoping you will have learned from my mistake."

Robert stopped for a minute before going on.

"I have, and will continue to my dying day, show you some guitar chord and licks, but I think my most important learning message to you is that you've got to put in the time and the practice, if this is what you want to do. Even if you decide to do something else, and I don't care if that is be a garbage man, a lawyer, a doctor, a farm worker, you've got to put in the time to be the best at what you do, and no short-cuts."

Just then the wind started whipping. The air turned cold. Diddley could see his breath. What was happening?

"Don't be afraid, young Didd. Just stay behind me. I had it in my mind that this might happen." Robert pushed Didd behind him, and he gratefully stayed there as they stood on top of an unknown grave marker, looking out and around as it got colder and the wind whipped more furiously.

Then Didd, with his own eyes this time, saw a shadow moving toward them. The shadow was hooded, just like Robert had described in their earlier conversation. Indeed, the hooded shadow floated toward them, moving quickly. The shadow became airborne and began circling him and Robert Johnson. Didd thought he just might pee on himself, but was able to hold onto Robert's back as they watched the circling darkness above.

The clouded image flew over their heads for a couple of minutes, as if sizing them up. It finally landed about 10 feet away and Diddley could see that the shrouded image was just like the Mr. DeVille that Robert had described. The hooded figure was walking toward them although he wasn't really walking but floating. He got within 5 feet of Robert and Diddley and stopped.

"Robert Johnson, it's been a long time since we last met," said the figure.

Diddley couldn't see the face beneath the hood, or notice what one would think of as a regular face with a set of eyes, nose, and mouth. Nothing moved. He could just hear the words.

"Yes. It has been awhile Mr. DeVile," said Robert. His voice shook, but was firm and clear.

"And to what do we owe this visit?" said DeVile.

"My friend here, young master Diddley Squatt, is just embarking into this mystery called life. The young lad definitely is fit for musical talent and is destined for genius. I have watched him since he was a little Squatt and I've seen the respect and care he treats every individual, every animal, every living and breathing thing. Everybody knows he has a good heart. As for me, I am nearing the end of my time here on earth. As my last chance of redemption for all the bad I have done, I wanted to bring Diddley into some of my past experiences and maybe show him a different way. I want to show him the truth."

"And what was wrong with our way?" said the shroud. "You became successful and your dreams were fulfilled, were they not? You experienced fame, women, the world, what else is there? What was wrong with your truth?"

"The truth is that yes, I sold my soul to you many long years ago. I became successful. I've enjoyed many of the guilty pleasures the common man yearns for. That was great, but I got my greatness the wrong way. I've had very, very, very few peaceful nights because of the manner I got my talent and fame. When my head hit the pillow at night, my sleep was not peaceful or restful. I don't want that for young Didd," said Robert forcefully.

"Alas, you have regrets, Robert Johnson." **Mr. DeVile laughed in such a manner that shook the valley and bounced off the canyon walls, "Well, it is far too late for that, my friend. Your soul served me well during your stay on earth. After listening to your music, you turned many a man and woman into a drunken soul and they've done some very dastardly, sinful deeds. Your juke joint extravaganzas led them right to me. You've been of great help." The shroud let out a deafening belly laugh that shook the graveyard.**

"Well, Mr. DeVile, today is my day of reckoning. Today I get my comeuppance. Today I hope to regain my soul before I meet my maker, and young Didd is my conduit and my redemption going forward. Yes, I've played honky-tonks from Texas to Mississippi to California, all over the USA. I've slept with more women than I can count. I've drunk whiskey from the Atlantic to the Pacific, but with a conscience – and it ends tonight!" Robert dropped to his knees and covered his head. Mr. DeVile, the shroud, whatever, floated over and stopped directly in front of Diddley. Didd once again tried to look into his face, but there was absolutely nothing there.

The shroud spoke:

"So, you think you have some sort of musical talent, and you don't need my blessing -is that correct? And your name is what, Diddley Squatt?" The shroud laughed again, its bellowing cackle rolling out over the headstones. "What kind of silly ass sissy name is that!" His laughing continued; shaking the trees and causing leaves and branches to fall. Madness.

"You don't know who you are dealing with young blood," said Mr. DeVile, "for standing in your presence is the DEVIL himself. Mr. DeVile is my earthly name. I think you have gotten yourself into some deep devil doo-doo listening to my past comrade, now apparently a traitor. Robert Johnson has not really helped your situation. You don't know the whole story?"

The shroud spoke as he continually circled Diddley.

"I have been responsible for many an earthly man's good fortune; way too many to name. They all come to the Crossroads and give me their souls. In return, I give them fleeting earthly pleasures, but their souls belong to me. They think they are gifted, but they aren't. They all BOUGHT their gifts, and that is no way to earn respect. It's a quick fix, and 90% of earthlings would give their souls for the quick-fix. There is no other way. So Diddley Squatt, what the hell are you going to do? BOW TO ME and give me your soul

and you can embark on your trek with your wretched guitar, your measly harmonica, and I will make you famous. Obey my command or the world will never hear of a Diddley Squatt!" Mr. DeVile waved his arms and shook hell fire from the skies above us as they turned a fiery red; churned with ominous clouds.

The trees shook like a hurricane was upon us.

Diddley became absolutely terrified for only the third time in his life. First? He remembered back to the first time when he was bullied and laughed at in grade school because of his name; secondly, when Glorendous left him before he could make her his first ever girlfriend and left town; and third, right now, in the presence of this very scary Mr. DeVile. Standing here in this darkened night, Diddley figured this was the most afraid and scared he had ever been in his life -right now!

But then he began thinking about his life- and the progress he had made from where he began, and the scariness began to dissipate. His thoughts became "what do I have to fear? I came from nothing, and love found me. And every time I've had fears; love found me. Why not now? If people have put their faith in me and feel that I may be somewhat special, I'm not going to let them down. I'm going to stand tall regardless what happens!"

So after his pep-talk to himself, what are the first words out of Didd's mouth?

"Um... um... um... um... um... um...
um... um... um... um... um... um... um...
um... um... um... um... um... um... um...
um... and um."

Diddley couldn't get the courageous words
in his brain to transfer to his mouth – He was just
so terrified in this darkened, chill filled cemetery!!
Um was all he could mutter. The bullying couldn't
compare to tonight's fright. Sabrina Tuggers?
Nothing! Herbert Hebert? – a joke compared to
this. This was the real deal.

**Upon the silence, Mr. Deville said
laughingly to them both:**

**"This is really sad! You two came all the
way out here and this is what you present- a
sad sack of an old, probably dying Robert
Johnson and an even sadder young squirt with
the despicable name of Diddley Squatt – quite
pathetic for you humans?"**

DIDDLEY EXPLODED!!!!!!

"NO! I STAND WITH ROBERT" said
young Didd. He felt an unknown courage
pouring from his frame. Didd himself was
shocked, he never knew he possessed the courage
to stand-up and speak this way.

"I will practice, and practice, and practice,
and pray, and practice. I want to earn my gifts
and talents by the right way. I don't want your
quick cure. I don't want a false magical cure to
my life. I want to earn it!"

"I want to make people proud, even though I was born with the name Diddley Squatt. And by the way, if you think the name Diddley is a "sissy" name, I want to let you know that I stand with all the sissies of the world!"

Diddley took a breath and continued.

"I had a conversation in a men's bathroom awhile back about so-called queers and sissies-and women possibly liking only women and men liking men; nowadays they are known as homosexuals – and I say let them alone. I've met some of these different people since that conversation, and they are the most fun and peaceful and gay people ever. I say let them be -let's get on with "let's being"… that's it – let's call them "lesbeings" and move forward. The world is always evolving; when will we realize we are all God's children – and just choose love instead of hate. It takes energy to hate something, and I'd rather use that energy practicing my guitar and loving people and animals instead of thinking of fast ways to get around life's obstacles."

Diddley continued:

"I've met people from other backgrounds and races that have been bullied and discriminated against because of the color of their skin, or are refugees or immigrants. My Italian friend Marco, and his lovely family who treated me as one of their own, told me stories of how he and his family were called "dagos" or "wops" – yet they got through it like all my black brothers and sisters called "niggers"; like my bullied white friend Pryor. Through it all - we all stand tall!"

So yes... Robert brought me here for a reason – and I won't betray him. I know him better than I know you, Mr. DeVile, and love and righteousness will win in the end."

The dark figure leaned back into a deep laugh and his **VOICE DARKENED.**

"You have no idea what you are talking about, you young fool. People will always hate those who are different. I've made it my life's work to make people uncomfortable and hate those who are different. You should know that just by being black. Has your God friend helped you black folks? You can't even go certain places; eat or stay at hotels; hell, even drink at certain fountains- because of your skin color. However, young Diddley or whatever your strange name is, we are getting off the point and I have other places to be and other souls to win. As for Robert, he's dying, you idiot. Why bother with anything that he says. Dying people will tell you anything, believe me, I have heard it all."

DeVile paced, circling the two waiting in the dark.

"I need some new souls, and remember, you came here to me, after all. I can indeed make you rich and famous. Think about this very moment, it may be the most important moment in your life and you don't get a do-over. You can have any worldly pleasures you

wish: **Women. Fame. Money. Liquor… you name it. Travel the country playing your stupid harmonica and "geetar" beginning tomorrow, with just the snap of my fingers. Why in the world would you want to take years practicing to learn such crazy lessons. And my only request, just a lousy soul?"** laughed DeVile.

"As I said - I still stand with Robert," said Diddley.

Mr. DeVile stilled, now visibly ANGRY.

"Well, that's not going to happen, Doodley, Dudley, whatever the hell your name is!" Mr. DeVile snapped. **"You can't get past me and the souls that I possess."** The shroud snapped his fingers and like bats in the night, tiny shrouds started swarming around them like flies around a dead catfish. Diddley was afraid, but held firm. The black shrouds, hundreds of them, grew larger and soon they lined up behind Mr. DeVile. **"You will give me your soul tonight young Didd; you can't get past us!"**

"I can. I have faith!" shouted Diddley as he pulled his harmonica from around his neck and began playing as loud as he could on the lower chords, near the low # holes. BLOWING LIKE NEVER BEFORE. The hills rattled from the bass low notes of the harmonica. Diddley and Robert dropped to their knees and Diddley played while as if praying. He then quoted one of his favorite bible verses:

"You, Mr. DeVile- are a false prophet. As I learned in church, 2 Peter 2: verse 1-3:

"But false prophets also rose among the people, just as there will also be false teachers among you, who will secretly introduce destructible heresies, even denying the master who brought them, bringing swift destruction upon themselves. Many will follow their sensuality, and because of them the way of the truth will be maligned; and in their greed, they will exploit you with false words; their judgement from long ago is not idle, and their destruction is not asleep."

"God is good. Got is great." Didd shouted.

Mr. DeVile grabbed his ears in anguish.

Diddley continued:

"EPHESIANS 6:11:

"PUT ON THE FULL ARMOR OF GOD, SO THAT YOU WILL BE ABLE TO STAND FIRM AGAINST THE DEVIL!"

"OH NO... NOT THE GOD WORD AND THE BLASTED BIBLE!

Diddley then blew again. Miraculously, Diddley's harmonica's music turned as loud as if the heavens were crowing. The low notes of his harmonica bellowed through the still air of the cemetery and surrounding hills.

Deville and his shrouds grabbed their ears as the notes vibrated louder and louder as they echoed from the hills.

In an instant, Diddley and Robert disappeared right in front of their eyes.

Unbeknownst to DeVile and his fellow shrouds, Diddley had hit the right chords and he and Robert had shrunk to an ant's size. LadyM was right on time. Didd and Robert hopped aboard, and soon they were passing Mr. DeVile right in front of his face, although he had no idea where they had gone.

"Where did they go?" shouted DeVile," you shrouded minions find them or you will have hell to pay!"

"Let's ride," said Didd as they rose from the cemetery. Soon they were on their way back home.

"I'll learn the right way. Thank you, Robert Johnson, for the lesson at the Crossroads," came Didd.

"You are welcome Diddley. You are indeed one strange young man. You are going to go far, and do it the right way. Please let me add a big, grateful thank you to Ms. LadyM, a beautiful friend to the end indeed." said Bobby, holding on tight to Lady M.

"You are welcome my new-found friend," said LadyM, flashing those eyelashes while zooming back home.

"GOD IS GREAT," all 3 said in unison as they jetted off.

A couple of months later, not long after the Robert Johnson/ Crossroads episode, Robert Johnson indeed did pass away. While the funeral was at the Rundown First Baptist Church, the wake was held at the Copp-A-Squatt Inn. What a wake it was! The whole hotel was full to the brim, both inside and out with all the various folks that knew and loved Robert. Musicians, pimps, ladies of the night, gamblers, farm workers, and factory workers. BBQ pits in the back yard of the Copp-A-Squatt spewed sweet smelling smoking barbeque ribs, chicken, goat. There were tables of potato salad, greens and turnips, sweet potato pie, black eyed peas, and all types of desserts.

In the middle of the celebration, all the guests were told to meet in the backyard. Momma Squatt stood on a crate to speak.

"Ya'll put your drinks and plates down for a second and listen. We want everyone to have a good time; but Robert did leave one last request. Diddley Squatt, my grandson, please come up here. Also, Tiffany the Epiphany, please bring out what Robert left for Diddley Squatt."

As Diddley moved up front, he noticed Tiffany cradling a guitar and a small case in her other hand. She handed the items to Momma Squatt.

"Diddley, Robert left you a couple of his favorite possessions. All he said was "he'll know what to do with them." She handed the guitar to Diddley. Next, she handed him Robert's sunglasses case, with his famous sunglasses inside. All those in the crowd applauded.

"Thank you, Momma," said Diddley sheepishly.

The party continued. The liquor flowed; stories of Robert's life were told, and retold. The ladies in their short dresses weren't cold; everyone was having a time of all times for Robert Johnson's send-off.

Diddley kept holding the beat-up guitar, but in his eyes, it glistened as if heaven shone on it. He held onto that guitar case and put that sunglass case in his front pocket.

Now that he officially owned a guitar of his own, it became his most prized possession in his life. He indeed began practicing and strumming the guitar that very night, just like he promised.

CHAPTER 7

Virginity & Other
Important Life Lessons

The vigor's; studying and all, of high school continued. After this summer, Diddley was would start his 11th grade year – he was now 16 years-old. During the summer, Didd continued to help out at the Copp- A-Squatt, doing all the various chores to keep the place decent (cleaning this and that; replacing this and that; running errands for his/her and whomever – the Copp-A-Squatt was in need of constant upkeep). But wherever he went, whenever possible, he now had his guitar gig-bag strung over his shoulder and wore his Bobby Johnson sunglasses. In between his chores, he practiced the guitar, practicing some chords Robert had showed him before he passed, and picking up pieces of songs he heard on the radio that blared constantly at the Copp -A-Squatt; songs like "I Want a Bowlegged Woman;" "The Honeydripper"; "Lawdy Miss Clawdy"; "Stagger Lee;" "Shake, Rattle, and Roll." Diddley had a ball trying to learn the songs on his own.

Diddley learns the Hambone

One summer day, Didd was told to go to Rundown City's downtown area, to the Rundown Express store, on his rickety bike and pick up some supplies for the Copp-A-Squatt (flour, bleach, lard, bread and eggs.) He had a basket on the front of his bike and had become quite efficient in bringing supplies. And you guessed it, he had his guitar in its beat-up cloth covering – wrapped around his back -his ever-present guitar. As he entered downtown, he happened to see the crowd circling somebody in front of the train station. The Rundown Train Depot was as hot a spot as any in town- it was the only place in the city for departing and incoming parties. As he cycled closer to the party, he saw young boys doing this strange slapping and flapping of their knees and chests. As he closed in, he realized why all this was happening; this dapper older man dude– wearing a hip crisscross dapper zoot suit; hair slicked back; alligator clean shoes on his feet. Obviously, he wasn't from Rundown City and probably just stopped for a short time or changing busses or trains or something – but he was holding court. Diddley scooted up close on his bicycle, and he clearly saw this sharp out-of-towner – sparkling white teeth in an endless smile- having fun and teaching the kids this new dance of his.

"This dance is called the "hambone" said the stranger. "My name is Otis Johnny- and this is the newest dance craze!"

Didd was mesmerized as Otis threw a hump in his back; squatted on his back hunches, and began to hucklebuck, as Stew the Harmonica Fool (*real, real* old-time dude, maybe in his 90's, who frequented the Rundown Train Depot and played for pennies for the comers and geezers was jamming away on his harmonica – Stew is so old he taught Nate the

Skate how to play the harmonica.) Meanwhile, Otis Johnny was having a ball – alternately slapping his thighs, licking his lips, slapping his chest, crossing himself between his groin and his legs. I mean this guy was on fire he was so rhythmically going at it!

Didd jumped off his bicycle, tugged off his guitar gig bag and wrapped his arms around his guitar, and started jamming with Otis Johnny – right in tune and on time!

"That's the Hambone ya'll. Get used to it, and just remember that Otis Johnny, from New Orleans, first brought it to you!"

After their jam, Otis Johnny said "where is that mean young cat that was playing that mean guitar lick – THAT BOY IS BAD!!" He met Didd and shook his hand, telling him to keep at it and if he was ever in town someplace and Otis Johnny was playing – he was welcome to come on stage and jam. It was a huge thrill for Diddley to be recognized for his early learning guitar skills.

The local kids kept practicing the hambone as the departing train pulled up- and Otis Johnny was soon gone and history. However, Didd practiced the hambone at night in his room, and was developing thoughts of how to incorporate the syncopation of the beats into his guitar playing and how it all related to music, timing, and drum beats. Didd's musical mind curiosity of various genres had just lit fire, and he wouldn't forget the hambone and how to use it in the future.

Diddley Loses His Virginity

Might seem like he waited longer than necessary for his first sexual experience, but Didd was busy concentrating on his schooling and guitar practicing/playing. While it was apparent Diddley liked school, he enjoyed more so the guitar and music.

In the 11th grade, at now 16 years-old, he was fascinated by math and all that it entailed. And, of course, there was science, along with his affinity and kinship with all animals – young and small. While he loved learning about science stuff, the one part he didn't like was where the class dissected frogs and other animals. Didd hated to see dead animals, even if it was so that students could learn a frog's hamstring muscle or a rabbit's inner left ear. He brought his displeasure to a teacher's attention, who at least tried to comfort him by stating "we first look for good roadkill – we won't kill healthy animals."

Also at the start of 11th grade, the fascination the girls had with him continued to grow. Didd, with his patched jeans, worn black and blue t-shirts; cuffed pants. Didd was blossoming into a very, very handsome young man and as the high school years passed more girls took notice. His face was beginning to sprout signs of facial hair... and Didd's hair became curlier and longer... he was easily more noticed than other kids his age because of his different look. No more bullies, so Diddley continued to earn the reputation as a very peaceful dude just going about his business. With books in his arms; the girls **loved** that he had those books in his arms; that tiny harmonica he had since he was little, the tattered leather chain still fashionably enough to fit around his neck; and the ever-present Robert Johnson signature guitar gig bag swathed around his other arm and neck. Didd had taken to wearing those sunglasses that Robert also left him; they looked just as cool on him as they did on Bobby (may he rest in peace.) All the young girls smiled and nodded when he passed by -oh my!

One night, Didd was making his regular rounds through the Copp-A-Squatt floors, picking up and emptying trash cans here; replenishing bars of soap, toilet paper, fresh towels, magazines, cigars and cigarettes there. While he didn't vacuum, or replace the sheets – he did just about everything else to clean the rooms

He passed Chastity's room which he loved! Her room was always afresh with the latest floral scents and she liked to keep the window drapes pulled back to show the beautiful moon and stars. Didd pushed his moveable cart (full of all his required replenishments) and moved throughout the room; replacing this; emptying that; unaware anyone else was in the room, when he heard a very sweet voice:

"Young Didd, my favorite young stud." He looked over and was surprised to see Chastity laying in her bed, a night gown strung loosely around her body, sitting in the dark bed with one knee-up, one knee down - smoking a smoldering cigarette. She was as foxy as foxy can get.

"Sorry Chastity. I didn't know you were here" said Diddley as he sheepishly emptied the trash can by the drawer.

"Oh no my young brother, fate brought you here today. This is your lucky day, time, and place. It's fate taking place my young Didd. Please close the door," said Chastity in that sexy, sexy throttle of hers.

Didd sheepishly closed the door and then just as quickly shyly backed himself up against the door.

Chastity rose from her bed and slithered over to Didd. She was like a snake in the desert heat – all warm, slithery, and shiny.

"My real name is Essie Mae Davis. I was born and raised in the cotton fields of way-back-yonder Alabama. You and everybody around here know me as Chastity, but that is just a name I made up for myself. Chastity is a much more inviting and sexy name, wouldn't you agree?"

Young Didd nervously bobbed his head in agreement.

Chastity continued: "I came from nothing and have very little. While I have no material possessions to give to you like a harmonica or a guitar, I indeed do have a gift that I want to give to you. It is time. I've been watching your progression from child to man, and I think today-now-is the right time. Plus, judging from your body and that bulge in your jeans, you definitely already have an idea of the gift and possession I want to give you.

Didd started sweating profusely; he couldn't stop the sweating. Was the sweating due to the heat? Are you kidding?

"Say something young Didd," said Chastity as she moved off the bed, quickly closed and locked the door, and was now directly in his face; make-up on; legs and body pressing against Diddley - a beautiful vixen if ever there was one.

"I... I... I... I think this may be the best gift I will have ever received in my life; better than all those prior. I know secretly I want it to be!"

"You've earned it my young friend," said Chastity as she took Didd by the shoulders and pushed him to the bed. "But before we go any further – I need to know something and you have to tell me the truth. You are 16 years-old, is that correct?"

"Yes Ms. Chastity – I am 16 years old my last birthday. I would never lie to you," said Diddley.

"I know you wouldn't young squire. I just had to make sure you are of what they call "legal consent age" in this state before we go any further. You are indeed legally at a man's age. Momma Squatt preaches law-abiding and I wouldn't want to get her, and more importantly ME OR YOU, in any trouble. So, we are good to go," said Chastity. She continued:

"You have indeed been a trusted true fiend, an unbelievable good soul and helped out your grandma like no one else. So today I give you the gift and pleasure of sex; and I know you will take it as just the next stepping stone toward this journey

I know God has for you. I am just so happy that it is me presenting you this gift! Let's take our time. I'll show you what to do."

She hovered over Didd, he laying on his back where Chastity pushed him. Chastity raised his t-shirt off his abdomen over his head; threw it to the ground, then unzipped his jeans and helped him remove his pants. Didd was left lying on the bed as Chastity continued removing the last of his clothing – down to his socks. Chastity then leaned down and kissed Diddley's forehead; the softest, sweetest kiss he had ever received. She then removed her nightgown over her head, and she was now naked up top looking into Diddley's excited eyes.

"Touch me here," she said as she took his hand and lead it to her left breast.

"These are breasts, and combined with a tender touch, and a sweet, loving kiss in the right place, they are the gateway to a woman's initial sexual feelings. It's Ok to explore them, but just remember to be gentle and loving" she said as she moved down close to Diddley. She was now straddling/sitting atop Didd; just sitting there with an occasional moan, raising and lowering her arms; as she allowed Diddley to caress and explore her lovely black body with his fingers. Didd's fingers were no longer trembling, but assuredly rubbing and stroking.

"Now kiss my breasts gently" she said as she leaned over and placed them right over Didd's head. His first kiss was an awkward smooch, but soon his manly instincts took over as he ever so gently sucked her nipples- first her left – then her right; and he quickly didn't need any further lessons about the breasts. He also continued to feel a strong erection down below.

Now make no mistake – Didd had masturbated before. He had first heard/learned about "jacking-off" at school gym class a couple of years ago. And, yes, he had tried it a couple of times, but the feeling couldn't compare to what he was feeling at this very moment. Chastity continued to slowly move up and down and moan occasionally – giving Didd confidence with each small moan.

"Now, reach down and gently feel my body part under my panties, but be careful. This area of a woman's body is very sensitive. This is a woman's vagina. Let me give you some lotion to begin with," said Chastity as she reached over and grabbed some lotion from the bed stand. She rubbed it onto Didd's fingertips; and then took his right hand and lead it to her golden spot. "Rub gently… rub slowly… nothing harsh… and feel the moisture as you begin to make my natural reactions begin," she said.

Didd slowly began rubbing Chastity with the tips of his fingers, slowly rubbing and caressing, and indeed he could feel Chastity's breathing escalate. As he explored her inner self, his erection gained strength second by second. There was moisture gaining in all areas. Next, she moved to Didd's ear and swirled her tongue around his ear; her breathing alone almost made Didd explode.

"So now you think we are ready, right? No - there is one important lesson I need to teach you; and this may be the most important lesson to remember before any sexual relationship you have in the future."

Chastity grasped Diddley's open palm and pressed a small paper packet into it.

"This is called a condom – or the more common name you may have heard is a "rubber." It is used for the protection, for both parties, to prevent the spread of what are known as sexually transmitted diseases – the most common of which is called gonorrhea. Your grandma has a rule that every one of the Copp-A-Squatt customers MUST use a condom before engaging in sex. It leaves both parties safe, and prevents unwanted pregnancies."

"I've heard of condoms, and I've sound some while doing my chores", said Diddley, "and we've actually talked about it a little bit in Health Class. Although I've never used one, I'm pretty sure I know how to put it on, "said Didd embarrassingly.

"You never fail to amaze me," laughed Chastity.

Didd ripped off the covering and was ready lickety split.

"Now it is time. Let me take my panties off and guide you in."

Soon, they had switched positions. Chastity had switched to lying on her back and Didd was quickly on top straddling her prone body. She reached down and grabbed his penis – a thrill of its own – and lead him into her vagina. She continued to coach Didd, advising him to move slowly and to enjoy and savor each second. Diddley obeyed every instruction! His eyes soon shut - and nature took over. Didd imagined he was flying high above in the clouds with this beautiful, soft and warm, woman underneath him, as he gently stroked, and stroked. IT WAS TOTAL HEAVEN!!!

Well… one can imagine the rest… no need to go further.

Soon. Afterward. Diddley was outside Chastity's room. He stopped and leaned against the hall wall. Flying??? Making himself small????? Talking to animals??? None of those earlier experiences could compare to his first time experiencing sex!

"I am one lucky young man," was all he said as he pushed his cart down the hallway.

Young Didd was no longer a virgin – another lesson learned and conquered.

CHAPTER 8

Diddley Meets His Best Friend Ever

Diddley Meets Sylvester (Sly) Squinter -the Squirrel – Friends for Life

A couple of weeks after Didd lost his virginity, and before his senior year is set to begin, the young stud is sitting on his favorite sawed-off pine tree stump in the Copp-A-Squatt backyard. He's leaning back, quietly picking at his guitar, eyes closed -not really thinking about anything. It is a beautiful fall evening, not yet night, and the stars have just begun to showcase. With his chore's all done; homework done, it is the time of day he relishes most. Like a lot of the homes in Rundown City – the backyard doesn't actually have a fence to let you know the backyard per-se has ended. The grassy area just starts running into the forest woods and beyond the woods? Just more forest and more forest woods-more woods. The smell of the woods is stronger than the smell of the collard greens.

So Didd is casually picking when he hears a:

"chirp... chirp"

near his right ear. He slowly opens his eyes and there sitting on a pine branch is this little squirrel; little thing, sitting up on the branch just as square as a soldier at attention. He's looking Didd square in the eyes. He has a pine nut is his paws eating away like a human might on an ear of corn. He never takes his eyes off of Diddley's eyes.

Now this is the funniest looking squirrel Didd has ever seen. He's not as big as other squirrels – as a matter of fact he is definitely smaller, except for those huge piercing eyes. And, it appears he has flat back, kind of like wings on his back? In all other ways, he resembles a squirrel.

Diddley doesn't want to spook him and have him run away, so the two of them just sit there in silence for at least five (5) minutes, the squirrel gnawing away – eyes front- and Diddley doing the same.

…FIVE MINUTES…
Silence
Silence
Silence

Finally, Didd says "How are you doing today, my squirrel friend?"

"Well I'll be. I thought you'd never ask!" says the squirrel who stops gnawing for a second.

Diddley almost falls over from shock on the directness of the squirrel's answer.

"You can talk?" asks Diddley.

"Of course, I can talk you ninny, how the heck you think we talking now? How you think we get things done in the animal world… jeezzz!" says the squirrel. "All animals can communicate – it's just that you humans don't take the time to listen. Why would our world be any different than yours?

Some of the other animals told me they have already discussed this with you – but I guess we will go through it again. You humans think you are so smart. I've heard your theory about animals – including those with opposable thumbs -compared to those without. I just came over after a bet with LadyM the Ladybug. She said you were different, and said that if I was patient I might actually have my first conversation with a human. She said you would be the one in this area of the woods and I could distinguish you because you'd have a tiny harmonica around your neck and maybe be plucking this thing called a "gee-tar." The squirrel continues nibbling on his nut.

"Well, this world indeed continues to amaze me day by day "Didd says with a laugh and a stinging chord on his guitar.

"This world is 'nuts' – no pun intended" said the squirrel, "and thanks for finally opening up and trusting me. It is indeed an amazing place, and today is indeed a special day. I mean I never thought I'd actually talk to a human and have him understand me and vice-versa. I'm glad I took this chance and approached you. Most of my other animal friends, including my squirrel cousins, said I was a 'nut'- pun intended-to trust you. They said you would probably pull out a pistol and shoot me and I'd end up on Momma-Squatt's stove as a Sunday dinner!"

"I would never, ever, kill a species of life, regardless of human or animal - that's just not me" said Didd earnestly.

"My my. But that's exactly what Percy and LadyM said you'd say. I guess they were correct" said the squirrel.

"So, I guess introductions are in order. My name is Diddley Squatt," said Didd as he held out his hand to shake the squirrel's paw.

"My name is Sylvester F. Squinter, but everybody just calls me Sly" said the squirrel as he dropped the nut and stuck out his tiny paw. The two shook hands (paws.)

"Sly – why did you take the chance to come out to me specifically?" asked Didd.

"Well, I just figured since I don't really have any family left in this world, what do I have to lose? My mom and dad where killed when I was little - probably ended up as a stew featured on one of your species dinner table. Anyway, I was born in the northern part of the United States. You can probably tell I look a little different than the other squirrels around here. That's because I am different. See - I'm actually a flying squirrel. I don't know of any other flying squirrels down here in the southern part of America. But before my parents died, these other bigger squirrels came north and pretty much adopted me and brought me down south. I lived with a lady who I called Grandma Squinter. She raised me from my formative years. She got old and died awhile back. I miss Momma Squinter. No brothers or sisters; I'm what you folks down here might call an immigrant to the area – but I just call it home.

One thing though. I was bullied and teased because of my size and my wings. The other animals called me "Sly the squint" and "Squinty Pinty Paws" – all kinds of names. Lucky, some other animal friends came to my rescue, and I just learned to get along by talking to others in the forest world.

"Wow... that's amazing!" said Didd excitedly," sorry for your loss; but your story sounds EXACTLY similar to what happened in my life? My mom and dad may be alive someplace, but I was left and raised by my grandma Momma-Squatt, similar to your story. I was bullied like crazy because of my name – similar to your story. Imagine that. We have similar backgrounds. We may even be kindred souls."

"What's a kindred soul?" said Sly as he picked up his nut and resumed chomping.

"It's a term I recently learned/earned from some of my human friends and others. It just means that we were destined to meet and become friends. As we've already discussed, we have many similar traits; upbringing, kindness and respect of others being the chief traits. The other night while thinking about the words kindred souls I thought of a song. And then meeting you today? The rest of the lyrics just now popped in my head. I've got to play the song now or I will forget."

Didd stands and starts strumming his guitar to a funky beat. He stops and does the hambone he learned from Otis Johnny – and then resumes playing and starts singing his newfound song:

> **"Me and my animal friends**
> **We get along like kin**
> **The world is truly one**
> **If you don't look outside- just look within**
> **Just step aside and feel the fun**
> **Let the earth hit you with the sun**
> **I met my squirrel buddy**
> **Met him on the fly**
> **My name is Diddley**
> **And his name is Sly**

To Didd's surprise, Sly spreads those funky wings and flies off his tree branch onto a closer branch right by where Didd is playing his guitar and singing. Sly starts singing:

Met this dude named Didd and immediately had this feel
LadyM suggested he was good, and it would be a good roll

> **At first I thought I might end up on his grill**
> **But after talking – he told me we were kindred souls**

They both then finished the song with this last chorus:

> **His name is Sly**
> **My name is Squatt**
> **He doesn't need to know why**
> **I don't need to know what**
> **We are both kindred souls – this is what we got**
> **This is the Legend of Sly Squinter and Diddley Squatt!!!**

Diddley and Sly break out in huge belly laughs and Diddley can't believe that Sly chimed in on his song and new exactly the lyrics to sing. But the surprises weren't over. Sly slides down the branch, and hops onto the neck of Diddley's guitar. He continues sliding down, and with his hind legs hanging from the top of the guitar, throws his paws down and begins plucking the guitar in the likes Robert Johnson would have been proud! Sly is breaking off a tremendous guitar solo; bending notes; scratching like nobody's business, his updown little fingers moving at light speed strumming/plucking - all in tune. Sly then completes his amazing solo and slithers back up the guitar from whence he came. He sits back on the branch, picks up the pine nut, and resumes to chew like nothing happened.

"That was amazing" is all that Didd can say…" WOW!"

"You don't think I didn't do my due diligence and didn't do some reconnaissance on you and others before I came down and talked, do you?" says Sly slyly. "Reconnaissance is a word we animals learned long ago -it just means we did some studying before moving and acting. I think it is a military term," said Sly. "Spent many an hour in the window by your room; watching your every move. I would then move upstairs and watch your friend Robert Johnson while just sitting there chewing on a nut; not only watching him screw Delilah and Chastity – both beautiful women with tremendous bodies I must say, but also watching him practice his guitar. It looked so interesting. See, squirrels – both flying and regular- have great minds for remembrance. I was just fascinated with guitar playing. So, when I saw you bring out your guitar, and you made me feel safe, I just had to try it out."

"You knew Robert??? This was his guitar. Sly - I'm sure he would have been very proud and amazed at your guitar playing. He took me to the Crossroads and I learned some important life lessons from him; better life lessons than guitar lessons. A lot of folks wanted this guitar – but he left it for me. So, if you still watch in the windows, please help me watch over this guitar," said Didd earnestly, "and you can jam with me anytime you want."

"You got it my newfound friend" said Sly.

"That was certainly fun Sly," said Diddley.

"Backatcha dude - tremendous fun. And it was so much fun talking to a human species for the first time. I certainly hope we can talk again," said Sly as he dropped the last few remnants of his nut and stuck out his paw.

"This is the newest hip way to shake hands. It's called "giving 5," said Diddley as he held Sly's paw and then slid it back cool as ice water.

"I like that!" said Sly, "I know where your room is. If you hear me scratching at your one window – it's me. Let's help each other through this thing called life."

"Agreed. I better see you again Sly -my kindred soul" Didd said with a laugh.

"Oh. One last thing before we part. I should hip you to the code words we use in the forest. I imagine it would be Ok for me to share this information with you. What we animals do in this Rundown Forest when we see an unfriendly human coming and it may get dangerous- we alert each other by shouting out our code words," said Sylvester.

"Sounds like a good idea. I don't want anybody to surprise us and for something to happen when we might be conversing. What are these secret code words?" asked Diddley.

Sly cups his small hands to his mouth and shouts out:

"HOOTY HOOT… HOOTY HOOT"

"We got the idea from the Wise Old Owl who has been around forever. You are the only human to know this important information – but I know I can trust you. So-if for some reason we need to cease our conversation – I'm sure you are aware people might think you are crazy if they ever saw you talking to an animal – just yell it out and we stop immediately till the threat passes. Try it out, "says Sly.

"Hooty Hoot… Hooty Hoot" says Didd.

"C'mon… you can yell louder than that? laughs Sly.

"HOOTY HOOT… HOOTY HOOT"

"There… you got it now," says Sly. "Remember now, this is just to be used around me or any other animals you may be conversing with during emergency situations in the threat of danger.

"Outta-site!" says Didd.

"Chow dude – gotta go find me a lady friend" says Sly as he scampers up a pine branch and is soon lost in the forest.

"It just keeps getting better!" says Didd as he slings his guitar around his back and heads back to the Copp-A-Squatt. Time for dinner.

Senior Year of High School

Diddley made senior year. He is now in the 12th grade-17 years-old. Diddley, he of the secretly flying; the feats of smalling; the talking to animals; the hamboning - through it all, young Didd had grown into a handsome young man! Hair continually longer- curly natural type hair – and yes, still, most of the time wears those pants that Momma Squatt bought him called "blue jeans." Diddley loves blue jeans – and refuses to throw a pair away if they get old and ratted; he has one of the girls at the Copp-A-Squatt (Delilah, Chastity, Epiphany, or Delilah) sew patches into any holes or rough areas He also continually plays his guitar and has gotten quite good, as a matter of fact, wherever he goes (bathroom, dinner table, to the store; or just walking down the street) he continues to have his Robert Johnson signature guitar strapped around his back – as well as his ever present harmonica and when outdoors- his sunglasses. One thing he now realizes, for sure, is that Rundown City is just not quite the "hotspot" for a gunning musician.

Sure, he continues "busking" on Rundown street corners (that's where musicians play on street corners for free – throwing out a hat for change and tips.) Diddley plays some Saturdays at the Copp-A-Squatt–all his "family" there loves to encourage him as he practices his standard or original songs in front of small, yet live, audiences… honing his craft. He also plays occasionally in neighboring cities, continuing the tradition of laying down a hat or open guitar case for nickels and dimes folks will occasionally throw his way. This is his shop during his senior high school year – after school and on weekends; his "set-up" after his chores are done at the Copp-A-Squatt.

Back to senior year. While Diddley enjoys school, and plays on the football, basketball, baseball, and track teams; and he is a member of the science club, a very good student academic wise; and he is a popular student especially among the girls. However, he just knows in his heart that he is not college material and won't be attending college. He feels his furthering education will be done in juke joints/clubs/street corners - and probably not in Rundown City. As for college – he has no one to really turn to to give him any advice; especially from any adult males. Black folks were not being overly accepted into colleges at that time anyway. Scholarships – no way... schools were granting very few scholarships to black students. Actually, Diddley hated depending upon anyone for help; his only family was Momma-Squatt and the characters at the Copp-A-Squatt, so his support system was limited. Momma's chores at the Inn did give him a sense of work ethic and being needed; and he grew to understand the meaning of responsibility, and he felt he learned to earn his meals and the place to drop his head at night. Indeed, he learned how to work and *earn* what he needed to survive in this world and the sympathy or gravy train – any type of welfare, never applied to him. In the end though, because of financial and other reasons, he just knew in his heart that college would not be a viable option for him, and he had accepted the fact.

Senior year flew by. Graduation day finally came that last senior year. Diddley sported his green and black graduation gown that day – Rundown City High's colors. As the seniors began marching into the rundown Rundown auditorium, Didd had his ever-present-guitar gig bag slung from his shoulder.

The school's Principal, Principal Spikings, understood Diddley felt naked without his guitar bag- so he was allowed to carry it wherever and it was accepted by all. Momma Squatt, now in a wheelchair for events like today, Chastity, Delilah, Tiffany the Epiphany, and Destiny – all rose to their feet and let out a yell when they marched in. I'm sure folks wondered who these fine, yet older women, were yelling for at this grad night. Yet, these five Copp-A-Squatt regulars were the only folks left from Diddley's childhood – most, if not all, the other colorful characters were now deceased and most buried at Rundown Cemetery.

And of course, Diddley did have his most special character/ close friend at his graduation to help him celebrate. While he was sitting on stage, in his usual little pouch stationed at the top of his guitar gig bag -his best friend Sly the squirrel was tucked inside and listening/watching all that was going on. See, Destiny, who over timed learned quilting and sewing techniques and became quite the seamstress extraordinaire - had lined the pocket/pouch with extra warm linen. Didd lied and said the pouch was needed to help keep his sandwiches warm and cozy, but it was Sly's home when traveling with Diddley. Sly was hidden, warm and cozy – and could actually go deep throughout hidden pockets in the gig bag if necessary. Diddley could now take his squirrel friend with him anywhere, and most of the time went nowhere without his best buddy. The top pocket area was so close Sly could talk to Diddley without anyone seeing or realizing his existence.

Principal Spikings began calling out the names. When he got to the "S's" he asked those with the last names who began with "S" to stand up. It wasn't that many – but they all stood up. Principal Spikings called out the kids with the last names like Sanders... Skillings... Southers... and then "Diddley Squatt" – EVERYBDOY IN THE AUDIENCE,

MAINLY OLDER PARENTS AND BROTHERS AND SISTERS NOT AWARE OF WHAT DIDDLEY HAD GONE THROUGH THESE PAST 17 YEARS -BROKE OUT IN LAUGHTER. WHY? JUST BECAUSE OF THE NAME DIDDLEY SQUATT.

Sly heard stuff like "is that his real name Diddley Squatt?"

"Diddley?" Let alone Squatt for a last name?" said others as the laughter continued.

Diddley was of course use to the ridicule, so when his name was called he just strode onstage, proud as ever and used to the laughter.

"Didd", Sly whispered as Diddley walked across the stage to accept his diploma." I am so proud of you my brother. From all indications, this graduation thing appears to be a big step in a human's life- and for you to share this experience with me is something I will always remember and hopefully tell my grand-squirrels one day. And for them to laugh at your name -and you don't care? -damn you are strong! Squirrels don't have schools as you know it. We do teach our young how to hunt for nuts and berries, but that's about it," said Sylvester.

"Glad you are here on this special day Sylvester" Diddley whispered out loud," things wouldn't have been the same in my life if I never met you. I always knew animals were special – and you helped prove it."

Didd accepted his diploma – flipped his tassel from one side to the next (as was a custom); smiled the biggest and brightest smile; and raised both of his arms in triumph.

The crowd seemingly changed its attitude; somewhat suddenly realizing that this young man appreciated and accepted his weird name of Diddley Squatt. Then the crowd started chanting:

"Diddley Squatt"
"Diddley Squatt"
"Diddley Squatt"

As he stood center stage with his arms raised, looking out at the proud faces of Momma Squatt, Chastity, Destiny, Epiphany and the others -Didd whispered over his shoulder to Sly:

"I'll show em Sly... I'll show em that names don't matter... it is the person... I'll show em!"

"You mean WE will show them" said Sly, "I will be there with you all the way."

That night, after graduation, there would be a celebration at the Copp-A- Squatt.

CHAPTER 9

High School Graduation Night

The Copp-A-Squatt was both immaculate and funky at the same time for Diddley's graduation party. The front and back yards were cut and mowed and the front of the motel glowed with its neon lights flashing all sparkling and new. The backyard was lit up with lights and tables and chairs for any amount of overflow - and this was just the front and backyards. Let's move into the interior of the famous Copp-A-Squatt:

The parlor: Remember, when one first enters the famous Squatt, you walked through the doors to find the parlor, which tonight was polished to a tee; the wooden floors with a sparkle and shine that hadn't glittered that much in years! All the bookshelves and cabinets- spit-and polished like a President was coming. Pictures of dignitaries that had frequented the Copp-A-Squatt at one time or another, like Jack Johnson, Cab Calloway, Bull Moose Johnson, Jackie Robinson, Jesse Owens, Thurgood Marshall, Wiley Branton -all acclaimed blacks who had passed (or allegedly passed?) through the Squatt. While the black "dignitaries/famous folk" didn't mind if the pictures went up – the important/ famous white folks who had also passed through and visited the Copp-A-Squatt, Momma

Squatt kept a rule to honor their request that their particular pictures could never be publicly shown. As the story goes, years ago, when these white dignitaries made their requests, Momma Squatt sighed "No problem; I believe in honoring peoples wishes regardless of color as long as they pay like everybody else!"

The parlor held between 60-100 folks. At about 7pm. the pimped-out Cadillacs, Sevilles, army jeeps started arriving. Tonight, there would be a mixture of the usual folks: johns in zoot suits and Stacey Adams spit-shined shoes with their ladies sitting on their laps dressed to the nines in black knit stockings, high heels, fake furs and slit-ted dresses, and red lipstick; and anybody else who wandered in. It was an open night.

About 8p.m. Momma Squatt, was wheeled to the front of the parlor where she was front and center stage. She stood with the help of her cane and waved it above her head signaling the masses to stop with their salty stories; halt the beer bottles and clinking glasses of bootleg scotch and other hooch simmers; turn down low the blues music blaring from the jukebox/ record player. Momma-Squatt began:

"My name is Momma Squatt – but ya'll know that. My husband was Doodley Squatt and we had one child, a daughter named Jackie Squatt – but most of ya'll know that too.

(laughter)

It all began a long time ago. Doodley wasn't a perfect man... he had his devils like anybody else; but he worked hard and we were able to scrap together our savings and start this here hotel we are sitting in today. Overall, Doodley was a good man, born with that funny first and even funnier last name - but he never let that bother him. Doodley left this earth waaaaayyyy too soon. I'm sure he would be proud of his only grandson Diddley.

Anyway, my daughter Jackie got herself pregnant by some wayward soul named Deangelo or something crazy like that- and had a baby some 17 years-ago. She named the baby Diddley. Jackie knew immediately she wasn't cut out to be a mom. She left baby Diddley with me, and he's been with me, and a lot of you, at the Copp-A-Squatt ever since.

Young Didd graduated from Rundown High School earlier today, and we are here to honor and celebrate this accomplishment. When he gets up here to speak I think he has an announcement to make that, unfortunately, will leave us sad. He's becoming a man now, so I'll leave that up to him to tell you."

(the room goes completely silent at this last sentence)

Momma Squatt continues:

"Listen… I'm getting way up in years and Lord knows I won't be here too much longer; that's a given – just ask those no longer here today to celebrate who helped to raise Diddley, but this applies to many of ya'll out there too… even you younger folk. But on this night – tonight- let's wish my grandson Diddley Squatt some hearty congratulations for graduating high school and wish him the best in his future. Young Didd has been nothing but a godsend; the boy has not given me ONE day of grief or caused any trouble. All he is done is help and be a good grandson.

(Momma Squatt starts to tear up)

God couldn't have sent me a better person - and I'm not ashamed to be tearing up - God blessed me and Rundown City with this boy who has grown into a man.

So Diddley... this is your night. You know how much we love you. Everybody please raise your glasses.

(the entire house raises their glasses)

May you find your calling the Lord wishes for you – and be successful and prosper – and understand that you always have a home here in Rundown City (everybody clinks their glasses together and let out a yell.)

Ok Diddley. Time for you to come up here and say something son," says Momma Squatt as others help her back toward her seat in the wheelchair.

Now, while Diddley was indeed on the Rundown City debate team – that was one thing; you know, speaking before his peers? This, however, was completely different, at least in Diddley's mind. Diddley was very, VERY, shy about speaking in public to those older or just the public in general. Simply put- Diddley had no choice and this was his very public coming out party, right?

So Diddley rises, wearing a pair of his best patched blue jeans; a t-shirt with a crude picture of Bobby "Robert" Johnson scrawled across the chest; a nice grey blazer that someone had left a long time ago -and his crusty boots. Didd, now graduating, had his hair growing out into the new "natural" style that was exploding across black America. He had chin stubble hair that he hoped one day would develop into a beard. To say the least, as Diddley sashayed toward the front of the raised parlor he was a different cat – hip, newness; a handsome young lad leading the way; and of course, he had his guitar gig bag slung around his shoulder. Yes, sunglasses on, and the ever-present tiny harmonica slung around his neck. And- last but not least – he had his latest accessory/accomplice with him; of course, his little flying squirrel friend Sly was in his familiar and safe pouch- hidden to all but accessible to Didd.

Didd finally made it to the front of the parlor and removed his sunglasses before he began. He reached into his back pocket and pulled out his trusty, leathered and olding journal. He flipped through it and quickly picked out some basic stuff to say. This was the same journal that Bobby had originally given him years ago, and it definitely came in handy during his lifetime:

Diddley began:

"I'm not the greatest speaker – and in the words of my grandma – "I'm sure ya" ll already know that!"

(Laughter throughout the parlor)

"But I just want to say thank you all for coming out and celebrating this accomplishment with me. First off, I want to acknowledge the lady most responsible for my being here. That is of course Momma Squatt. Momma, I was so little when my mom left, so I have very few memories of her; but I do have glimpses and remembrances of my mom saying how she loved me dearly. I've tried to think about why she might have left me so early, and I haven't come up with any clear answers. But over time, I have resolved my feelings to the point where she must have done it for all the right reasons. I have absolutely no malice or hard feelings toward my mom. I love her. She was obviously a loving and smart person if she left me with Momma. So, Momma Squatt, it goes without saying, that I love you dearly and owe everything to you. Let's give my grandmother another round of applause.

(Applause all around for Momma Squatt-who wipes away tears)

Also, I have to thank the ladies of the Copp-A-Squatt who pretty much raised me like I was one of their own; that would include the beautiful ladies of four known as Chastity, Destiny, Tiffany the Epiphany, and Delilah. Without the guidance of you 4 ladies, I would not be standing here today. You 4 changed my diapers, cleaned my butt, sewed my clothes, sewed my patches; helped me with my homework. You taught me things from since I was first crawling around the Inn, then learned to walk and talk; progressing through childhood; through puberty (Diddley winks at Chastity knowingly... she puckers her lips and blows knowingly kisses right back at him.) So - let's have these four special ladies stand and please let them know how much they mean to me.

The four ladies stand and there is raucous, raucous applause for these four popular Copp-A- Squatt ladies. They are all dressed in tight revealing dresses – showing off all the assets god bestowed on the lasses. Age has done nothing but enhanced their beauty! They blow kisses at Diddley and around the room.

"There are also a couple of men I need to thank but they are no longer with us. That would first be Nate the Skate from way back in the day. Nate was responsible for providing me with the first of the musical instruments you have rarely seen me without – my trusty mouth harmonica (he grabs the harmonica around his neck and kisses it.) Then of course there was RJ... or Robert Johnson... he taught me the beauty of guitar music and to keep a daily journal – both of which I am never without. Both of these men taught me how these instruments and music itself could be used to escape during difficult times. These 2 instruments have been crucial to me in my development thru life; and consequently; the reason why

I must now let you all in on a secret Momma Squatt alluded to earlier.

THE ROOM GROWS EERILY SILENT

I will soon be leaving Rundown City very soon - maybe not forever – but for now – to venture out into this big world and see what awaits this dude named Diddley. Maybe I can make my living as a musician; maybe not. But I hope you all understand when I say I need to try.

(The crowd remains silent at this news- we hear some cries and groans)

Without question, I also need to thank all the other colorful characters I have met at the Copp-A-Squatt and Rundown City these past 17 years – some who helped my upbringing positively and others through negative deeds but who unknowingly were also helpful - folks like Rusty Bhutt, Herbert Hebert, Priscilla Hotbody, Sabrina Tuggers, Percy Possum, GG Prince, Cecil the Beetle, Sun House, Marco Valentus, Glorendous, and Stew the Harmonica Fool – to name a few. My time here has been nothing but a learning experience; listening to all your stories and loooooooooooooooooooooong tales over Momma-Squatt's barbeques and affairs; over the ribs, the greens, the biscuits and gravy, the red beans and rice, the ham hocks and pork chops; fried okra, grits and hog head cheese; chitlins and smothered steak… yum… I'm gonna miss it all.

Before I end, I think ya'll also know I like to write from-time-to time. I wrote a little poem in my journal called "When I'm A Copp-A-Squattin" and I'd like to leave y'all with it. Here goes:

"When I'm A Copp-A-Squattin"
Pork chops and biscuits,
Gravy and every type of liquids
Red beans and rice,
God's blessings and nice vice,

When I'm a Copp-A-Squattin
Everything and Everybody is a happenin and stompin
It Ain't no Jive or Jivin
Cause these are my peeps and we's a rompin!

Ups and all kinds of downs,
Smiles but also some frowns
Dancing, shimmying and all kind of shaking
b-b-ques, fish frying, and birthday/holiday baking

When I'm a Copp-A-Squattin
Everything and Everybody is a happenin and stompin
It Ain't no Jive or Jivin
Cause these are my peeps and we's a rompin!

Kisses, hugs, and perfumed lasses
Bootleg liquor in red cups and glasses
Bid whist and poker, blackjack and dominoes slingin
Booties shaking/salmon frying and a baking

Robert Johnson and everybody a singin
Party all night – and in the morning your head will be ringin
But none of it matters… pause to cause
I' guess what I'm saying is I love all of Ya'lls

cause

When I'm a Copp-A-Squattin
Everything and Everybody is a happenin and stompin
It Ain't no Jive or Jivin
Cause these are my peeps and we's a rompin!

(applause)

"That's it. Thank you everybody (but Diddley then hears Sly yelling at him from his pouch)

"HOOTY HOOT... HOOTY HOOT"

"Diddley you forgot all your animal friends. You must tell them thank you. Look out the window - many of them are outside and I told them you would be leaving. Please tell all our animal friends what they meant to you – this is a big hooty- hoot moment!!!"

Didd jumps to attention again:
"Oh, wait a minute please... I forgot one special group to thank. Before I forget, I must also give a BIG thanks to all my animal friends and tell them how much they have meant to me over all these years. Some of my most calming days have come from sitting in the Copp-A-Squatt backyard and just listening and looking at all the dogs and cats, squirrels, birds, snakes, lizards, moths, hummingbirds, and possums, that I've enjoyed viewing as they went about their business; especially my squirrel friends. May you forever be plentiful in fruits and nuts of all types! Thank you all!!!"

(Diddley winks at Sly – Sly winks back.
They were finally able to get in a hooty- hoot minute)

Diddley exits the stage to great applause and starts walking down the center of the parlor as all the folks part and pat him on the back and high-five him from both sides.

The party continued through the night. The party ended up being one of many legendary parties in the annals of Copp-A-Squatt parties. One side note; late into the night (it was actually early morning) – young Didd was coaxed into tasting his first ever sip of bootleg liquor. Now, he had a couple of sips in the past; and immediately threw up unlike he had ever threw-up/upchucked before. But this moment was momentous because he was leaving, and since he was being egged on, he had to try it again. Didd sipped some alcohol, and of course barfed all over the floor. THAT WAS IT – he wasn't sad - it just re-affirmed what he knew in his heart; that alcohol and drugs of any type did not suit him. Didd would never do drugs or drink alcohol!

A couple of days after the party, Diddley packed this huge "duffle" bag – a gift from Destiny- with all his clothes that could fit; t-shirts, patched jeans; his one good black suit that was suitable for any "formal" occasions; mountains of underwear; his extra boots; soaps and toiletries and toothpastes. He was able to fit quite a bit into his huge new duffle bag. When he hit the porch to leave Rundown City, he had his duffle bag wrapped around one shoulder – his guitar gig bag slung around the other (Sly sleeping in his pouch of course) and all his other regular accessories. Today he wore his navy colored navy issued "P" jacket some john had left at the Copp-A-Squatt (as mentioned earlier, folks were always getting drunk and leaving clothes, especially coats, in the Copp-A-Squatt parlor closet. Momma had a rule to not touch these items for two weeks; and if no one came to recover their items after two weeks – they were fair game for Copp-A-Squatt employees.) The "P" jacket was a nice and timely pick up for Young Didd.

Chastity, Destiny, Tiffany the Epiphany, Delilah, and Momma Squatt drove Diddley to the Rundown City Train Depot. Didd figured he would make his first extended ride out of Rundown a train ride instead of the more popular bus; what the heck. As he got out the car, he purchased his ticket and moved to the boarding area. Momma Squatt grabbed his arm.

"We took up a special collection last night when you were outside throwing up, and let me just say I'm glad that evil liquor and you don't get along. Anyways – God Bless-and here is the collection we took up to help you get started."

She handed Didd an envelope. Didd looked in, and to his surprise found mountains of $20's, $10's, $5's, and 1's. He was shocked.

"About $200 dollars," said Delilah… "we counted it. We hope this will help you get started with your dreams."

"WOW", said Didd, "that's a lot of money!" Indeed, $200 was a lot of money in those days and times. Didd took the envelope, folded it, and stuffed into the inside pocket of his P jacket – safe and secure.

"I got my eyes on it!" said Sly.

The train was approaching -the whistle blew.

"WHEWWWWWWW… WHEWWWWWW!"

Didd then silently went down the line of his most cherished and only family… Chastity first. Tears welled in his and their eyes.

"Be good… and shock the world" said Chastity. "You were always special. The Lord has something good for you" she said to Didd and kissed him tenderly on his cheek. Her tears flowed.

"Do your thang, Young Didd" said Destiny "your destiny is your destiny; and remember that you do have family who loves you," she kissed him on his other cheek as Tiffany and Delilah got in their last kisses.

Finally, Momma Squatt was last in line. They looked into each other's eyes; Momma finally spoke:

"Master Diddley Squatt. My only remaining family (tears break her up.) I just want to leave you with these words, which are you are so special to me! How could I possibly know that 17 years back, when my only daughter knew she couldn't care for you and wasn't ready to raise a child, and she was correct, that she could leave me with such a gift. I had first maybe thought to myself this could be a burden, but I quickly learned you were a joy instead. Child… not **ONE** second have you caused me a problem - not one second! You need to know I have never regretted taking you in. You think you were the lucky one? We were the lucky ones! Me -Rundown City - all the folks at the Copp-A-Squatt.

TEARS GALORE

But I understand you must go out into the world and seek your calling, the world awaits you. So, while my tears run because I will miss you, they are also tears of joy and happiness because I'm so damn proud of my grandson and I know you will follow God's will and do good. I know God will watch after you.

The last thing I want to say is… is that Diddley Squatt is a good name! So, go out and show em something Diddley Squatt!!!"

Momma throws her arms around Diddley's neck as they both cry and kiss. Diddley holds and kisses Momma Squatt like never before – truly genuine.

"ALL ABOARD" yells the conductor. Diddley lets loose - throws his luggage on the train and jumps on-board, and then leans out the door as the train slowly starts to depart – as he offers his departing words to his family/friends:

"I promise you I will make you proud. One day I'll return to Rundown City and we can all rejoice together. I love you all!"

The train picks up steam… Diddley hanging out looking at the 4 ladies and Momma Squatt – all with tears. The train starts slowly… picks up speed; more speed. Diddley hanging out the door looking… and then they all become specks.

CHAPTER 10

Diddley Strikes out on His Own

It seemed like the train was going on forever. Diddley at first was wide awake looking at the scenery as the train moved from trees and country through little hick towns back and forth. After a couple of hours of wide eyed watching, he fell asleep. When he awakened later, he peeked in at Sly in his pouch spread out -and his good buddy Sly was still sound asleep. Sly was lying on his back on his wings – with both his front and hind legs in the air like a content puppy. Didd laughed.

The train trudged on for what seemed forever... hours and hours. Finally, the train stopped and Diddley heard the trainmaster yell out "Welcome to Dreem City."

Dreem City was Diddley's first stop after Rundown City; Robert Johnson and others had mentioned Dreem City to Didd and how it was indeed a good city to get started. Didd grabbed his duffel bag and gig bag with Sly still sleeping, and soon he was off the train. It was about 9pm. in Dreem City:

What a sight!

Lights... EVERYWHERE! The first sign he saw:

*"WELCOME TO DREEM CITY –
THE CITY WITH THE BEST KITTYS.*

*NIGHTLIFE, DAYLIFE, WORK & SCHOOLS –
WE DON'T SUFFER ANY FOOLS"*

Then onward down the street, more of these lighted signs:

*"ACME HARDWARE –
OTHERS DON'T- BUT WE CARE"*

'HOTELS, MOTELS, HOLIDAY INNS?

"WELCOME ALL – YOU ARE ALL OUR FRIENDS!"

Diddley had never seen such bright lights before.

"I think they are called "neon lights" said Sly, unexpectedly now awake, as Diddley walked along the sidewalk, eyes as wide as saucers, "I heard some crows in the forest one day discussing these "bright ass lights" they encountered in a city, and how much easier these lights make it to find food if you need a midnight snack. I'm sure these are those same neon lights."

But it wasn't just the lights. My god - cars of all types flooded by on both sides of the street, just a running and honking and flying!! Cars much shinier and much, much newer than cars in Rundown City - with names like Chevys, Buicks, Dodges, Fords, Lincoln Continentals, Oldsmobiles, Cadillacs, Studebakers. Shiny/flashy cars all over the place. Diddley was looking up so much as he walked down the sidewalk that at one point he stepped into the street and heard a:

"SCREECCCH" as a taxi almost clipped him.

"Get out of the street – young tourist son-of-
a-bitch!" the cab driver yelled sticking his head
out of the cab. He zoomed off. Businesses galore;
liquor stores (no more backwoods moonshine
in the big city); furniture, deli's/grocery stores,
clothing/shoe stores, cleaners/barber and beauty
shops; all types of stores. And of course, lots
of bars, BARS, dot the avenue as Diddley and
Sly made their way toward Dreem City's "First
Avenue." First Avenue was the name of the only
street that Chastity had given him – she said
she knew he could probably find a nice/not-too-
expensive motel on First Ave.

Artists busked on corners with saxophones
and trumpets; drums fashioned from empty
buckets; paintings - hats on the ground for tips –
as well as homeless folks with palms out-stretched
requesting donations. Women? Of course, they
were aplenty, scantily dressed and saying "want
a good time baby - I'll give you the best time
ever;" luscious red lips and thighs high. Didd of
course knew these types of women from his years
in Rundown City from his many years watching
the girls at the Copp-A-Squatt.

The streets of Dreem City were indeed alive. Didd finally
made it to the motel section of First Avenue and found a hotel
with rooms for $4 a night – or $25 a week; and figured this was
as good a price/place as any to settle down for now. He rented
a small one-bedroom flat and settled in; plenty good enough
for he and Sly. The room overlooked First Avenue below and

had a balcony outside the window that would allow Didd and Sly to crawl through the window and sit outside and view both ways down the street. Perfect!

Didd unpacked his few belongings – placing his various t-shirts, jeans, and underwear into drawers. He took out his cash envelope from Momma Squatt and hid it in one of his old rusty boots – a trick Nate the Skate taught him long ago; if somebody where to break in, they wouldn't think of looking in one of his stinky boots - right?

"Have you forgotten something; or better yet someone?" Didd heard the voice.

"I don't think I have?" said Didd kiddingly, "maybe some pictures and a razor?"

"Me - you silly human… damn Didd!" said Sly as Didd opened up Sly's pouch and he squirreled out and surveyed the room. Sly immediately headed to the open window and ran into the fresh air supplied on the balcony. He jumped on the rail overlooking First Avenue.

"I apologize Sly. I just got caught up in all the excitement," said Didd as he too moved outside to take in some night air. "I've never felt this much excitement and energy in all my life, and that's just from walking the 5 blocks to the hotel. Life is jamming!"

"Jamming? Where did you find that word?" said Sly as he shimmied along the rail of the balcony, then took off and glided/flew into the room and around/around giving it the proverbial one-over- then back outside to the balcony area.

"I dunno – must have heard it somewhere," said Diddley as he pulled a chair out of the room and placed it on the balcony; he quickly pulled his guitar from his gig bag and just as quickly joined Sly back on the balcony. He started strumming a tune… and soon Sly jumped on the top of the guitar neck and started bouncing to the tune. They jammed for a while before Sly headed toward the edge of balcony.

"Where you going dude?" said Diddley.

"Dude? dude?... where did you find that word? First "jamming"... and now "dude"? What's happening with your new vocabulary?" said Sly.

"I heard it on the street from one of the panhandlers heading here. Is there a problem?"

'No... just wondering... man... you are really listening to what's happening on the street. That's good my brother?" said Sly.

"MY BROTHER??? Now you are doing it – where'd you hear that from?" said Diddley.

"Same as you. Heard it on the street coming here. Humans aren't the only ones with ears you know?' said Sly chuckling. "I'm hungry. I saw a park as we were heading here. I gotta go seek some nuts or some green floral/green stuff. You know we squirrels have to eat our greens also for health reasons. But, before I go for the night, I gotta ask you some questions. While I am very excited that we left Rundown City, and have headed out into out adventure, I gotta ask - what is our plan man? What we gonna do my brother?"

'We are gonna do what Chastity told me; something along the lines of 'playing it by ear' I think she called it," said Diddley.

"Tomorrow morning, I, and I mean you and I, will get up early in the morning and head to one of the nightclubs we passed on First Avenue. I saw some signs saying they were auditioning for acts – singers and bands- which I assume I qualify. Chastity called it "pounding the pavement" looking for work. So - that is the only plan I have at the time; pounding the pavement and looking for work. While we have a few bucks, we have to make enough to pay the weekly rent, but I think we can do it. Then, we just go with the flow my brother..."

"I like your thinking young man," said Sly, "we animals have similar thoughts of just going with what God presents. Sounds like a plan. So, for right now – as I said - I saw that park awhile back so I can always find food. I know you got human food – but if you ever are in need of nuts and berries my brother, just let me know. While I can't help my human friend find a job or help clean or anything – you gotta know I'm here to help you in any way I can. I'm a flying squirrel; so, if you can think of a special favor that a flying animal might help you with – I'm right here willing and able.

We are in Dreem City my friend – so dream big! I'm here with you. While I'm out exploring Dreem City; for maybe even a Mrs. Dreem City Kitty of the flying squirrel nature if you get my drift – I'll catch backatcha in the morn."

"Be careful" said Diddley, "give me 5 before you go."

Sly and Diddley slap paws/hands…" that's dap" said Diddley," something else new."

Sly hit the balcony, skittered along the rail for take-off purposes, and ran/glided into the night.

Diddley moved some other stuff around in the room… yawned… moved to the bed and collapsed. He hit the lights; and lights out for the first night in Dreem City.

-------------------------------Click-------------------------------

Next day. Diddley is sitting in the office of J.J. Brohams – who is on the phone talking to another client. J.J. hires a lot of the musicians for the various clubs in Dreem City. J.J. – an overweight white man with thinning white hair – is dressed in a crumpling suit with suspenders a-glare; busily chomping on a cigar. He has a whiskey glass half full to the side of the phone; he is just jawing away with some promoter/performer

-huffing/puffing/and smoking as he bellows into the receiver of the phone:

"Don't care what that son-of-a-bitch says, he's contracted to play with us starting tonight and he better uphold his contract-starting tonight – or I will see that son-of-a-bitch in court and ruin his career. I better hear back from you in the **next 5 minutes** or you will be hearing from my lawyers. It's 11: am. – and you are on the clock until 11:05am… son-of-a-bitch!"

J.J finally takes a look up from his desk and quickly eyes Diddley.

"Godamn musicians. So, what kind of music do you play? What's your name? Am I reading this correctly? Diddley Squat? What kind of f'ing name is that?"

"I'm from Rundown City sir, and Diddley Squatt is indeed my given name. I know my name is different and awkward, but I actually think that could lead to a bit of an extra draw. Folks might be intrigued with the name, and even just come hear out of curiosity of the unique name. I play roots music sir. My guitar can be played acoustically or I can plug it into these great new amplifiers that are really becoming popular and musicians are starting to use. I play a little bit of jazz; some blues; some gospel; some of the newer stuff such as rock and roll -and even newer rhythm and blues/soul music that is becoming popular; swing - a little country; a little voodoo from this cat who taught me named Robert Johnson; then there's a little backwoods barbeque music that everyone seems to connect. Plus, I am working on many original songs of my own that I hope to play for the world. To put it in the best language possible, I can and will play just about anything that gets the crowd moving!" said Diddley.

"Hell… that was quite a description; I'm curious -play me something," said J.J. while again returning to his whiskey glass.

Didd pulls out his guitar and starts in on "Crossroads"- his signature Robert Johnson song - laying down some beautiful blues licks and chords. Didd sings a couple of verses to show off his growly, yet young baritone soulful voice. He plays for a good 10 minutes before J. J stops him.

"Not bad… not bad. I can see you have some talent but it needs experience" he says through cigar smoke," and by my watch it is 11:20am. Today is your lucky day Diddley Squatt. That son-of-a-bitch never called me back!" stammers J.J. He then says this through cigar smoke:

> "Young boy - you go on tonight at 9p.m.
> at the Dreem City Little Kitty. You can play
> for the next two weeks. If the crowd likes you
> we will see how it goes from there. Pay is $25
> a week plus tips. Any questions?"

"No sir!" said Diddley excitedly, "I'll take it." They shake hands and Diddley flies out the door before J.J. changes his mind.

CHAPTER 11

Diddley Plays his First Gig
– The Legend is Born

8:00p.m. Diddley walks up to the club on First Avenue and eyes the neon lights above. The sign says:

"DREEM CITY LITTLE KITTY"

The little club is nice and quaint – and features a little cat pictured under its name. Diddley walks in, is shown to the dingy dressing room. He sits, and before taking out his guitar, just captures the moment of being in his first dressing room preparing for his first professional gig. He then pulls out his guitar and strums a tune. Soon it 8:55pm. The floor manager pokes his head in the door and says "Diddley Squatt - you go on in 5 minutes." Sly pokes his head out of his pouch.

"Wouldn't miss this for the world" he says to no one while munching on a park nut.

8:59p.m – Didd sits behind the stage with a small curtain drawn in front of him. He can hear glasses clinking; folks making small talk; the jukebox playing its last song before the featured performer performs. Didd is wearing his patched jeans; a t-shirt with the name "Robert Johnson Lives" across the chest; his favorite beat-up boots; his newly "afrow-ed" hair in kinky but stylish fashion. Didd is handsome, laid back, and ready for his debut. The curtain opens. A voice offstage says:

"Ladies and Gentleman – please welcome Diddley Squatt."

(of course ---- slight laughter from the crowd when Diddley's unique name is announced,)

The house lights are dim throughout the club except for the microphone, chair and club guitar amplifier area where Didd is seated with his guitar strapped and ready. Didd's gig bag is on the floor near his chair – with Sly of course hidden in his gig-bag pouch; undoubtedly the best seat in the house. A subtle spotlight is trained on Didd in his chair. He stands up from his chair and pushes it back. He grabs the microphone stand and pulls the microphone to his lips and announces:

"My name is Diddley Squatt. I hope you like my songs. My mentor was Robert Johnson from Rundown City – where I am proud to say I was born and raised. I grew up in the Copp-A-Squatt Inn (laughter.) I am excited to play you some of my songs; some original; some you might recognize. I appreciate this chance and hope you like my stuff. This first song I wanna play is an original instrumental dedicated to the friend of mine mentioned earlier, now passed, name of Robert "Bobby" Johnson. I call this song *"Kindred Souls from the Crossroads."*

Didd then kisses the harmonica around his neck for luck – then moves to the guitar amplifier behind him. He plugs in his guitar chord and turns that amplifier baby to its highest volume. He takes his guitar, turns back to the audience, and starts slow at first… playing beautiful and majestic chords as if from heaven. He then picks up the pace as his licks get louder and more pronounced. Soon, he is shredding guitar licks that shake the Dreem City Little Kitty walls. He walks up and down the guitar neck playing blues licks and chords. The small crowd, at first hesitant - becomes attentive. The small talk ceases and clinking glasses are dispensed. Didd stops for a ½ minute of pure silence. He then restarts and moves into a wicked guitar solo – his fingers flying across the guitar frets as if the wind cries mary. The audience sits stunned in awe - they have never heard anything like what they are now hearing!!!

-DIDD'S LICKS CAROM AND BANG OFF THE LEFT WALL!

-HIS GUITAR SHREDS BOUNCE, SHRIEK, AND BOOMERANG OFF THE RIGHT WALL!!

-HIS SEARING STRING PULLING AND AMPLIFIED PLUCKING SCREAM OFF THE REAR WALL!!!

Diddly had brought an extra-long guitar chord, so he leaves the stage area and starts walking through the club, darting in and around patrons sitting at their tables; all the while not missing a beat. He contorts his body, breathing life into his licks. Diddley stops in the rear of the club, the spotlight following him, and just as quickly moves smoothly into a soothing gentle jazz mode; beautiful melodies lifting from his fingers and amplifier. The audience members close their collective eyes as they sway to sweet and mellow jazz groove. Didd moves in-between jazz; some swing; some blues… the crowd can only sit dumbfounded – but a good dumbfounded. Finally, after 10 minutes, he heads back to the stage front and hits a last chord and says into the microphone:

"That was for my kindred souls… thank you!"

Folks in the crowd are left looking around dizzily – as if in a trance… looking at each other and going "WHAT IN THE HELL? What in the world did we just hear?"

Silence
Silence
Silence

Then a lone clap… then another clap… another clap… another clap… more applause… and soon the entire club is standing and clapping like a crazy mob. Then Sly, with his amplified ears, hears comments from the audience like:

"I don't know what that was, but it was electrifying."
"Unbelievable… what was that? Was it jive? blues? Swing? Jazz? This new stuff somebody called rock? This new soul/rhythm and blues stuff? Exactly what do you call it?"
"Wow! I am going to write this date on my calendar – I think we have just heard a new sound and new artist. Someone and something new is brewing."

Didd moves back to his chair area and can hear clearly as Sly says:

"They like it!" yells Sly from his pouch as he pokes his tiny head up a bit and peeks out at the standing crowd applauding. "Keep em coming. Play em something where they can hear your voice - show em you can sing."

Diddley moves into a song he is very familiar with so that is no problem. He grooves into *"Smothered Steak at the Lake"* and once again the crowd sits mesmerized at his playing and his singing. Dude Didd is just killing it!

Diddley runs through an hour of material that is very well received; introducing each song with a sentence like "this is an original song I wrote from when I was sitting in the Copp-A-Squatt back yard, and I looked up and saw the squirrels and birds dancing. I jotted down these lyrics in my journal. I have a squirrel friend named Sly, and he stopped by with a nut or two and helped me compose the song."

The crowd laughs aloud at Didd's words; as if a squirrel could help write a song... PU -LEEEESSS!

At the end of his set Didd says "This is my first professional gig – and I truly want to thank each of you from the bottom of my heart for being so attentive and listening to my music. I hope you enjoyed yourselves and will come back hear me again. I have tons of music that I want to share with the world. Thanks again," and with that Diddley attempts to exit stage right, but then a crescendo of applause starts to build and some patrons even stand – in essence giving Diddley a standing ovation for his first professional performance. Didd stops and waves his fist into the crowd before leaving the stage.

The first person to greet him stage right is J.J. Brohams – cigar in one hand - shot glass in the other. He begins patting Diddley on the back.

"That was terrific... marvelous... fantastic... I don't know exactly what it was... but the buzz was terrific. Did you here that applause Didd? Young man we must talk. You can play in my club anytime, and for as long as you want; you definitely have the residency for the next 2 weeks. Take tonight and celebrate your achievement; but let's talk real soon like tomorrow morning. The Dreem City Kitty may have birthed its true first superstar!" said J.J. patting Didd on the back - smoke spewing out of his nostrils and mouth. Heavens.

"You did it Didd!" says Sly as Didd gathers his gear from the now curtained-off stage and walks out of the nightclub, "are we celebrating tonight?"

"Not tonight my squirrel friend. I want to send a wire back to Momma Squatt and the girls and let them know I have employment for now, and it looks like everything is going OK for right now. There will be plenty of time to celebrate later. Tonight, we send that wire; go home... say a prayer of thanks... and get ready for tomorrow's show. I will, however, stop at the grocery store and get you a fancy celebratory bag of nuts. Howse that sound?"

"Sounds like a plan to me" says Sly. That's exactly what Sly and Didd did.

The next day, on the front page of the Dreem City Gazette, is a picture of Diddley on stage with his guitar. The headline reads:

"STRANGE – YET HAUNTINGLY BEAUTIFUL – DREEM CITY KITY GIVES BIRTH TO SIR DIDDLEY SQUATT. THE MUSIC WORLD MAY NEVER BE THE SAME."

The next night's show is sold out... as is the next... and the next... for two solid weeks, the line is wrapped around the corner with folks of all ages/races/creeds/genders - trying to get in and see what all the buzz is about. Diddley signs on with J.J. for another extended week, but leaves his options open after next week. Ladies and gentleman - Diddley Squatt is a hit!

Back at Diddley's room. Diddley is sitting on the bed propped up with some pillows behind him -strumming his guitar-his trusty journal on the bed as he does the "possible" -jots down possible chords and possible lyrics for possible new songs. Sly sits near his feet, feasting on his favorite Dreem City park nut.

Outside the window, down below on the street, are some young girls that have discovered where Diddley is staying. What is strange is that they are both of black and white persuasion - young girls - and they are just hanging around hoping to get a glimpse or a conversation with Diddley before he leaves for his nightly Kitty gig. The newspaper recently coined a phrase of these girl fans calling them "groupies" or something like that.

"Groupies outside," says Sly. "Man, you have really started something. I am so proud of you my brother. I mean you did id Didd. Hey... wait a minute... I like that... jot that down as your next song..." You Did Id Did." Make sure I get writer's credit. You can pay me in pistachios and fresh cashews."

Didd and Sly laugh.

Just then comes the harried banging from some street workmen who have been going at it all day repairing the street. The beat they are making is quite funky. Didd and Sly stop and listen with their ears wide open to a:

Sledgehammer workman. Although a tad late at night, he is filling potholes and fixing the street. This guy is obviously experienced; banging into the concrete with an expert and rhythmically consistency. Hell, a professional drummer couldn't provide a better beat!

"Pow… chuh -pow
"Pow… chuh- pow
"Pow… chuh- pow
"Pow… chuh- pow
"Pow… chuh pow

After listening awhile, Sly jumps on the bed's headboard near Didd and says "ain't that a funky beat? I feel the need to spit something out; some sort of a gritty type of song with just a beat and very little music. Listen to this:"

*"This is the first rap of Sir
Diddley*

*and his bestest BFF friend called
Sly*

*It was created one night at Dreem
City Kitty,*

*Sly's the squirrel, and Diddley's
the guy*

*We looking to set the music world
on fire*

Start a new thing called rap

*We spittin some mean and funky
lyrics*

*Ya'll gonna fall right into our
trap*

*Life is a changing fast and
furious,*

*and you gotta move with the
times*

*So don't be afraid of this new
music*

*Pop your fingers and tap your
paws to these new rhymes*

Humans and Animals all together

Ain't we all about the same?

*Let's join together and make a
team*

Let's put everybody in the game

*So this is our first new song we
wrote together*

*Let's all hip and hop down life's
line*

*If ya'll just listen and follow along
to old Sly and Young Didd*

The world's gonna turn out fine!"

"That was great Sly! Maybe one day kids will start rapping to that hip-hop sound. You never fail to amaze me my little buddy. However, we have a long way to go my kindred soul – a very long way. Bobby Johnson warned me how a little fame could wreck your career, so let's take this thing slow. But I can't lie - I do believe we are on the right path, and Dreem City was definitely the right place to start. I hope I am making Momma and all the dudes and the girls of Rundown City proud. Momma said they did an article on us in the Rundown Gazette and she was so, so proud of us. We have to remember this is just a beginning - it's just the beginning. We've got to keep writing songs and we have to find a way to get a record contract and get some of our songs out to the masses; that's the latest craze - records and promotion. I think our selling point is the amplified music -the young kids love the loudness and the brashness. I'm sure we can help lead the way of electronic music. I think it is funky."

"Funky?" says Sly, "another new word you heard or made up. I like it though… make it funky!"

Didd laughs.

"We have our work cut out for us my little friend. And from the bottom of my heart, I must say none of this would be possible without your friendship and wise words of wisdom about how the animal and human worlds operate. I wouldn't want to be on this journey with anyone else."

Sly stops chewing, as a tear drops from his squirrel eye. Just as quickly, he returns to his nut – but not before saying:

"We are in this together until the end; we've just started. We have songs to write; licks to learn; both human and squirrel females to meet and mate with… and females… and females… and cities to visit and conquer… the whole world to conquer. And I too want to add- BACKATCHA DIDD- THANK YOU – for I too was blessed the first day I heard you in the woods. I know some of your closest friends have moved on for now. I'm talking about Pryor Richards… and Marco Valentus… and of course Glorendous. However, I, sir Didd, will be by your side forever – will never leave until the good squirrel God says it is time for me to move on - you can take that with a nut and believe it! I knew you were the chosen one/ my kindred soul. I knew it was safe to talk to my first human.

However, now let's open that over there on the table?"

"Over there?" says Didd, "what is it?"

"It's called champagne you nerd. That J.J. Broham's guy had it sent to the room. Pop that damn champagne bottle and pour some into my cup."

"You know I don't like to drink" said Diddley, "however -. maybe with my best friend present- I will try a little champagne for the first time."

Didd pops the champagne and pours some in his cup – and fills Sly's miniature bowl (Sly runs over and pressures Didd's pouring hand up so he adds more.)

Sly is at his bowl on the table – Didd looking at his little friend. Sly reaches up his paw and Didd reaches across and they slide hand across paw - the newest version of giving a high five – it is now called "giving skin."

Didd raises his cup: "To Sly – may we prosper and open up our new music to the world."

Sly: "To Didd – may we do all of what you just said, and continue to find the flavor and beauty of nuts all over this great country. Get ready world… this is just the beginning… and for all those who don't know Diddley – YOU DON'T KNOW SQUATT!"

-CLICK-
The end

Printed in the United States
By Bookmasters